BROKEN CHAINS

CYNTHIA JO TERRELL

ZAMIZ PRESS

FICTION / Christian / General

FICTION / Christian / Romance / Suspense

Special discounts are available on quantity purchases by corporations, associations and others. For details, contact the author.

This book is a work of fiction. Any references to events, people, or places are used fictitiously. Names, characters, places and events are products of the author's imagination, and any resemblances to actual events or places or persons, living or dead, is entirely coincidental.

Neither the author nor the publisher assumes any responsibility or liability whatsoever on behalf of the consumer or reader of this material. Any perceived slight of any individual or organization is purely unintentional.

DO YOU HAVE A MESSAGE TO SHARE WITH THE WORLD?
ARE YOU INTERESTED IN HAVING YOUR BOOK PUBLISHED?
VISIT ZAMIZPRESS.COM

Broken Chains / Cynthia Jo Terrell — 1st Edition

ISBN: 978-1-949813-18-0

CHAPTER ONE

Hollow noises crept into Jeremy's hazy awareness and transitioned to what he thought were voices. Spoken words danced on the margin of meaning. Confusion played on his senses, yet he had no fear. His lack of perception didn't bother him (though somewhere in the back of his mind, he thought it should) as he inched toward clarity. Clicks and humming noises hovered around the edge of his recognition. His eyes blinked at blurred images as he tried to bring them into focus. The figures were saying words; at least, he thought the sounds were words. Then the faces, yes, that's what they were, disappeared. He shivered beneath his blanket.

Hours passed as conscious thought strained to overcome confusion. Fragmented images floated in and out of Jeremy's mind even as he attempted to grasp them. Awareness came in snippets. He was lying in bed while his chest and head throbbed with pain, but he didn't know the reason. He fought to remember.

The shadowy figure of a girl appeared in his mind's eye. They were together somewhere, alone at night. He closed his eyes and brought the site into focus. Trees, a lake, blackness lit by a yellow moon, and a sky full of stars swirled in a misty haze. The face of the girl sharpened. It was someone he should know, but now she was alone. He waited as his thoughts became more lucid. It was a midnight picnic. Memories flooded his mind, but now he fought against them. Yet, they were relentless, demanding an audience.

Screams split the calm of the night as he raced down the dark path. Trees and branches jumped at him. Images of weapons, the agony of pounding fists, blood, and terror collided in his mind. A girl's voice cried out for him, mingled with the sounds of wicked laughter. His form sprawled under a tree next to the girl, who lay motionless. Hot searing pain ripped through his chest. Voices, like echoes, flitted in and out of Jeremy's consciousness.

"Oh, no! What happened?"

"Oh, Lord, help us. I can't feel a pulse. Call 911! Can you hear me? Please don't die. Hang on, Buddy. Hang on."

Then he heard only silence.

* * *

Jeremy roused a little and opened his eyes. "Who are you?" he said to a figure standing beside him. "Where am I?" A low moan sounded from somewhere.

"I'm a nurse," came a voice that sounded far away. The nurse was speaking, but her voice faded in and out. Jeremy understood some of what she said—stab wound, a hospital, and pain mixed in a jumble of other noises.

"Oh, really?" he mumbled. "The kind made from a knife? I don't know why." Jeremy's voice drifted off. He heard another moan and was surprised to realize it came from him.

The nurse was still speaking. Jeremy worked to clear the haze from his brain. He heard mumblings about pain medicine and packing a wound. After the words, he felt a sensation of some rope-like thing pulling his gut and pain that took his breath away. "Oooh!" He groaned and clenched his fists.

The pain cleared enough fogginess that the nurse's words began to make sense. He was in a hospital with a wound from a knife. He remembered a dream he'd had sometime before about a picnic and a girl. But it wasn't a dream. And the girl was Shannon.

The nurse was still working on him. She seemed to be pushing something in his stomach. It hurt, but not as much. "Shannon. Is Shannon here?"

"I'm not sure," said the nurse. "I will have to check. Is she a family member?"

"Yes." Jeremy closed his eyes to think about it. "I think so."

* * *

Each day Jeremy's world became a little clearer. He kept asking about Shannon, but he still didn't understand where she was. Maybe she had already gone home, but no, if that were true, she would have come to see him. She must still be in the hospital. Or maybe she was in a different hospital. Maybe her injuries were as bad as his. He wondered why no one had told him how she was doing. He thought he had asked about her enough times to get an answer. "Where's Shannon? Is she in this hospital?" he asked his mother when she came for a visit.

She flinched and wouldn't meet his gaze as if his words startled her. His mother shook her head, "No… no, she isn't, but don't worry about that now." She pulled the covers up around his neck and patted his shoulder. He thought he saw tears in her eyes before she looked away.

"Where is she?" Fear grasped at his throat as he choked

out the words. "Is… is she ok? I want to know." He tried to sit up, but stabbing pain forced him back on the bed. "Where is she? Tell me."

"No, honey," a sob caught in her throat, "Shannon's gone," she whispered, "I'm so sorry."

"Gone? What do you mean?" He gasped as he caught her meaning. No. There had to be some mistake. He must still be confused. Jeremy stared into the face of his mother, but her quivering mouth and wet eyes told him it wasn't a mistake. "No. Please. No," he cried. "It can't be. Please, no."

He heard another voice he recognized as his father's. "The paramedics did everything they could, but they couldn't save her."

Jeremy's head thrashed upon the pillow, and his eyes squeezed shut. "I tried," he fought for his breath, "I tried. I couldn't help her. Oh, my poor Shannon. Oh no. I'm so sorry. No, no, no. Where is she?" he cried out.

Marianne gripped her son's hand as he absorbed the unbelievable truth. She didn't speak, but her face told Jeremy there was something more. He stared at his parents with shocked eyes and fell silent.

"Let's go ahead and do it now, Frank," she whispered to her husband. He left and an anxious tension filled the room.

A few minutes later, Frank came into the room carrying a small bundle wrapped in a blanket. He caught his wife's eyes and breathed out a soft sigh.

"Jeremy, look." His father spoke gently and lowered the bundle closer to Jeremy's face. "It's Shannon's baby. Paramedics delivered her after Shannon died. We waited to tell you until we thought you could understand." Jeremy's blue eyes searched his father's face in disbelief.

Amazingly, he hadn't remembered Shannon being pregnant until now.

His father brought the baby closer. "Would you like to hold her?"

Jeremy rubbed his temples, praying he would soon wake up from this nightmare. He didn't want to understand, and his mind refused to believe that the baby was Shannon's. His eyes fell upon the tiny child. It wasn't a nightmare; he was awake. Or was he? "No, no. Please, tell me I'm dreaming," he begged. It was inconceivable, yet true. But it couldn't be. He covered his eyes with his hand, buried his head in his pillow, and drifted into oblivion.

Near where he lay was a blackness, a hole or pit of some sort. Crawling over to the edge, he peered down into deep darkness. A monstrous clawed arm thrust out of the pit and dragged him over the edge. Jeremy's scream caught in his throat and melted into a powerless whimper.

His fingers clawed into the dirt wall as the dragon pulled him ever downward. "You're mine," screeched the demon dragon as flames spewed from his lips. Glowing, hideous red eyes bore into Jeremy's, and sickening laughter echoed throughout the pit as he plummeted into the fire below.

Jeremy woke to his mother's voice. She grasped his shoulders. "Jeremy, it's ok. Wake up. You're having a nightmare." With blue eyes dark with dread, he succumbed to his mother's embrace. She held him like a child. His mother was right, except he wasn't *having* a nightmare; he was living it.

CHAPTER TWO

J eremy sat with his father at his family's kitchen table. He brushed his finger through his dark blond hair. "How do I get through this? I don't know how to go on." He pressed his fingers against his temples. "I can't find my way."

"Give yourself time, Jeremy. I don't have easy answers for you. I wish I did." Frank blew out a puff of air. "If I could take your pain away, I would. You have the ear of God. Lean on Him. Pour out your hurt to Him. Maybe see a counselor for a few sessions to sort things out and learn how to deal with your grief."

"I know, Dad." Jeremy bit his lower lip. "I know what I should do." He shook his head, "but I can't pray right now. I can't find any words."

"Then I'll pray for you." Frank took his son's hands and prayed for his strength to face life without Shannon and find hope and joy again. "Remember, Son, God knows your pain and wants to help you through it. He knows the torment of loss and hopelessness. He knows how it feels to lose someone."

"I know what you are saying is true. It's just difficult to understand right now." Jeremy released his hands and propped up his head with his fingers on his forehead. "I feel like I'm lost in a dark tunnel with no light up ahead."

"I don't always understand either, Jeremy. I can tell people all about the original sin and the fall of man, but when I get down to the reason for what seems like unfair suffering I still question. All I know is that God loves us and shares our sorrows. He will lead you out of the shadows of sorrow if you call on Him."

Jeremy stood, rounded the table, and touched his father's shoulder. "Thanks, Dad. I know your words are true, but it's hard to accept them right now. Please keep praying for me. Pray I'll figure out how to go on."

* * *

Jeremy sat in a black wrought iron chair alone on his parent's back porch staring blankly across the yard. His life had been easy for the most part, a life that hadn't prepared him for such intense sorrow. He worked at pushing his pain deep inside. He could hide from the hurt and anger, but the despair overwhelmed him.

Jeremy had avoided listening to or reading any reports about the events of the night of Shannon's murder. Even the news that the drug-driven thugs who had killed Shannon, "just to see what it would be like to kill," had been captured brought him little relief. Each one pled guilty to avoid the death penalty. Jeremy felt the need to hate them, but he couldn't muster enough energy. Everyone assured him that he was in their prayers, but his empty soul didn't care. People gave all the usual meaningless platitudes.

"We're praying for you."

"Shannon is in a better place."

And the most incredible: "At least you have your baby."

He felt nothing for the child, and he didn't need empty and powerless prayers. He only wanted Shannon. He didn't want her to be in a better place. He wanted her with him. Each night he prayed he would wake up and find it was all a dream, but every sunrise brought fresh heartbreak. People could pray all they wanted, but Shannon would not come back. She was gone forever, leaving him utterly alone.

Jeremy shoved any anger deep inside and determined to quit questioning why because it required effort he was incapable of giving. He went through the motions of living mechanically, barely noticing the passage of each day. Each morning, his only concern was to have the strength to make it through the hours until he could collapse into a fitful sleep often filled with harrowing dreams.

It had been six weeks since that fateful night, and Jeremy knew he had decisions to make regarding Heather. Shannon had wanted that as her name when they learned she was having a girl, and it felt right to honor Shannon's request. During the month Jeremy had been in the hospital, Heather had lived with Shannon's parents, and now she was staying with her sister's family. He'd had no desire to see the child since the day his parents brought her to the hospital.

Shannon's parents, and his own, encouraged him to let Shannon's sister raise Heather. She and her husband had two children and were willing to raise Heather as their daughter, with Jeremy being as much a part of her life as he chose. Jeremy had not objected, but neither had he agreed. His intellect told him that the child would be better off with parents who could provide for her, and his heart felt nothing. Even so, he thought he should see the infant again before making a final decision. He closed his eyes and tilted his head toward the sky as unfallen tears formed behind his eyelids.

* * *

Since he was not yet released to drive, Jeremy had called Shannon's mother and father and arranged for them to bring the baby to his house. His parents had thoughtfully left for the afternoon. He showered, combed his longer-than-usual dark-blond hair, and even shaved for the first time in several days. He pulled on jeans and a t-shirt and then sat silently in the living room recliner and waited.

Now that Shannon's parents were on their way, Jeremy felt anxious about seeing the child again. He was not sure he should, or wanted to, see her. Indeed, it had been a shock when his parents brought her to him in the hospital. It was unbelievable that she could have been born after Shannon died. He couldn't remember much of anything about the baby he had seen only for a moment in the hospital. Would Shannon be reflected in her face? Could he handle the pain of seeing her child? His parents were right. He was young and unsettled, and Heather would be well cared for by her aunt's family. He would see her once again and then give his consent for Shannon's sister and brother-in-law to become her parents.

Jeremy sighed at the doorbell's ring and shuffled to the door, "Come in, and thank you for making the trip."

"It's fine, really." Beth hesitated, finding his eyes. She clutched the infant close to her chest. "We want you to make the decision you feel is best."

Heaviness filled the air in the room. "I appreciate that." He needed to explain to them what he had only yesterday told his parents. "Please sit down. You need to know something about Shannon and me."

They sat on the couch and looked at Jeremy, waiting for him to continue. Lowering his eyes, his chin resting on his hands, he spoke in soft tones. "I loved your daughter, and I know you may feel anger toward me." He blinked his eyes rapidly but couldn't stop an errant tear that spilled out and traced the side of his cheek. "But what you don't know is that Shannon and I were married." He met Beth and Richard's stunned gaze. "We married secretly and told no one until Shannon became pregnant, and we had to explain to the school's chaplain."

"Married? You were married and didn't even let us know?" Richard's eyes narrowed with the question. He looked at his wife, and she returned his look of astonishment. "Why?"

Why? There was that question again. It was the same one his parents had asked. He didn't know how to explain. It was too personal, too private. He knew Shannon and he could have waited. They could have resisted the temptation to be intimate, but they didn't want to. Yet, they needed to keep their relationship pure before the Lord. Eloping seemed the perfect solution. They would keep their marriage secret and have a wedding when they graduated from college in two years. They hadn't anticipated Shannon's pregnancy or considered any consequences of the lie they were living.

"Why?" the question was insistent, "Was Shannon already pregnant?"

"No, she wasn't. We hadn't even been... intimate. I— we...," Jeremy's voice was barely audible, "We wanted to be together. At the time it seemed like a good idea. When Shannon got pregnant, she was afraid to tell you because we were still in school, so we decided we would wait until the baby was born." Jeremy lowered his head and wiped his hands across his eyes. "I'm sorry, but we did love each other, and this baby was conceived in that love." He breathed in deeply. "I thought you would want to know.," he finished.

With moist eyes, he looked up to see that they were both fighting tears, and the child, oblivious to it all, lay staring up at the woman who held her. Richard finally found his voice. "We're glad you told us. It does help to know."

"Would you like to hold her?" Beth held the baby out to Jeremy.

Surprised into submission, Jeremy took the child. Words eluded him as he gazed down at the tiny being. Tentatively touching her face, realization jolted him. "Oh," he muttered as he blinked his eyes. "Our baby." Jeremy gazed at her tiny face. This infant girl with big blue eyes was not just Shannon's baby. She was a part of him, too, a manifestation of his and Shannon's love. He could not drag his eyes away from her, and for the first time, he faced the truth. He was a father. Jeremy was amazed. This baby's spirit was Shannon's legacy. He could never let her go.

CHAPTER THREE

"**Y**ou're right. I don't know what I'm getting into." Frustration colored Jeremy's voice. "I just know that I have a responsibility to care for my child. I have to do this." Heather lay asleep on her father's lap, her head cradled in his arms. His parents sat across from him on the couch staring at their son, as if trying to understand his change of heart. Jessie, his tall, dark-haired sister, sat cross-legged on the floor beside Jeremy's chair.

Marianne shook her head. Jeremy didn't begin to know what it was like to raise a child. Her mother's heart ached for her son. She didn't want this for him. Her eyes searched her husband's face. "Don't you agree, Frank? It would be the best thing for Heather. She would have a mother and father." Glancing at Jeremy, then seeking her husband's eyes again, she continued, "Jeremy could still be a part of her life. But if he lets Shannon's sister and her husband raise Heather, he could continue his education and become a minister like he planned."

Frank's voice was gentle, "Jeremy is a grown man, Marianne. He wants to raise his daughter. We've always taught him to take responsibility for his actions. How can we tell him not to now?"

"But, Frank, you know this isn't right," she pleaded, her voice rising. What was her husband saying? Surely he knew this idea wouldn't work. Her mouth trembled, "He's too young. He'll ruin his chance to go into the ministry." That was his dream and her dream for him. He could get past this. Nobody would even have to know. It was ridiculous for him to endure this trial when he didn't have to. He couldn't possibly continue school and care for this child. Shannon's sister and her husband would be the best parents for that little girl. "You know I'm right."

As a child, Jeremy had always been interested in spiritual matters and had a special relationship with God. Marianne remembered an occasion when Jeremy was about eleven. She had been pulling weeds from the flowerbed and hadn't noticed him watching her. "You love Jesus, right, Mom?" His blue eyes were intense.

She looked up and brushed the dirt from her hands. "Of course I do. Why do you ask?" Jeremy smiled then. "I figured you did, but I just wanted to be sure. I want to be a minister just like Dad. He told us we could share God's love with our friends." His eyes sparkled. "That's what I'm going to do."

"You will be a great minister, Jeremy." She hugged him, and he smiled up at her.

"I love you, Mom. I'll be the best minister in the world—next to Dad." Flashing his disarming smile, he turned and wandered away. Marianne knew her son could still follow his dream if he would only listen to reason. She sought her husband's eyes. Frank looked at her and gave a slight shake of his head.

"Jessie," she said, imploring her daughter, "He'll listen to you. Tell him what I'm saying is true."

Jessie had listened quietly and now eyed her brother with troubled eyes. "Oh, Mom, I..."

"Hey! I'm still in the room. You're all talking about me as if I'm some wayward child." Jeremy rubbed his temples. His voice held quiet determination. "I am going to do this, and you can either support me or not. Heather is my child and I... I need her. She gives me a reason to try... to try to feel something again. I don't want to live without Shannon. I don't have the strength to make myself care about anything." He paused, drew in a ragged breath, and reached for his sister's hand. "I'm empty. I need to feel something." He bowed his head, and his mouth trembled. "Maybe I won't be the best father, but I have to try. Don't you see? I owe it to Shannon and our baby." Jeremy hugged the infant closer, her hair dampened by his tears. "I couldn't see before—I didn't understand. I didn't feel anything until I first held Heather. I know now. I have to do this." His tears fell freely as his blue eyes met his mother's brown ones.

Marianne crossed the room and embraced him. His tears fell on her shoulder while she held him and prayed for his strength. "God, help him. Give me the grace to understand." She knew then. She would help Jeremy raise this child in whatever way she could.

* * *

Jeremy's encounter with Shannon's parents went better than he had hoped. He explained his decision to raise Heather, and though they had reservations, they accepted his choice. Shannon's parents had only one request—that they would be able to be grandparents in the way they would be if Shannon had not passed away because they could not bear to lose their granddaughter, too. Jeremy intended to do that even before they asked. Heather needed a relationship with Shannon's parents. It would be a connection to her mother. He planned to attend church with Shannon's parents the following Sunday and spend the afternoon at their house.

* * *

Life continued. Jeremy spent the rest of the summer working at the local discount chain while his mom babysat Heather. In the fall, he would return to college to continue his studies. Loving his daughter gave him a purpose for living and cracked the surface of his despair. When the pain of losing Shannon threatened to engulf him, he concentrated on caring for Heather, knowing that he needed to be strong for her. Though his mother babysat Heather when Jeremy was working or at school, he fed, bathed, and rocked her to sleep each evening. When his little daughter cried out at night, he held her and cuddled her back to sleep. Jeremy's soul longed for healing, but he pushed his pain deep in the crevices of his heart, refusing to acknowledge it. Survival was his only ambition.

CHAPTER FOUR

J eremy hesitated after stepping out of his car. Maybe he shouldn't have come. The warm August evening threatened memories he didn't care to entertain, memories he had become an expert at ignoring. Here, though, in this desolate place, his soul was vulnerable. Caught off guard by the intensity of his emotions, he leaned against the car, struggling to fight off the echoes of that night, but this time they arrived with a vengeance, commanding his attention. His eyes closed as he lost the battle with his memories.

Shannon was usually carefree and full of fun ideas. Lately, though, she had been worried. Neither of them had been home since a short visit at Christmas when they had managed to hide Shannon's pregnancy from their parents. Everyone at Cincinnati Bible College knew they were married, and they had been able to convince the dean and president that they were married before Shannon became pregnant. Whispered comments and knowing looks told them that not everyone believed their story, but it didn't matter. Shannon was worried for a different reason. She was seven months along, and she would either have to tell her parents when she returned home or figure out how to stay there for the summer.

"Don't stay in Cincinnati, Shannon, I'll help you tell your parents. We'll just explain about getting married and they'll understand. I'll be there for you always." Jeremy put his arms around her, pulled her close, and kissed her sweet lips, marveling that he had found the perfect mate in Shannon. He had prayed a long time for a girl that he could love, and God had answered him with Shannon. She was beautiful, kind, and fun—everything he'd ever wanted.

Jeremy was glad he had gone along with this nighttime picnic idea. Shannon needed a diversion, and the starry spring night was warm enough for just a light jacket. Their friends had agreed to join them on the spur of the moment and were on the way. It promised to be an enjoyable night. The grassy area secluded by several giant shade trees was perfect. "Wait here, Honey. This is a great place. I'll go for the cooler and be right back."

Lugging the cooler over the wooded trail, he heard Shannon's screams, and dropping his load, he tore down the path. He bolted toward Shannon faster than he had ever run, but three men grabbed him, wrestled him to the ground, and beat him in the stomach and head. He fought with adrenaline-fueled fierceness but was no match for the drug-crazed men. Then, finally subdued, he watched in unspeakable panic and horror, powerless to save her. Her screams penetrated the night air.

The memory faded, and Jeremy found himself slumped over, his head on the door frame of his car. He must have been there for several minutes. "Please help me, Lord. I'm not strong enough to do this." With unsteady legs, he situated four-month-old Heather in her stroller and trudged down the path that took him to Shannon's resting place. In his hand, he carried a single red rose. Red roses had been Shannon's favorite. He dreaded this trip. Not attending the funeral because of his injuries, he had no desire to visit Shannon's grave after being released from the hospital. But now, the need to say goodbye and bring closure to Shannon's death compelled him to come.

It wasn't difficult to find. As Jeremy stood before Shannon's grave with the wind gently lifting his hair, pain surged from the pit of his stomach and drove him to the ground. He knelt before the headstone, and his quivering fingers traced the letters that formed her name on the cool surface. "Oh, Shannon," he whispered. "I'm so sorry. I failed you. I couldn't save you. God!" he shouted to the heavens, "Why did you take her away after you sent her to me?" Grief engulfed him as he collapsed to the ground. Why had God deserted him? Was this a cruel punishment for the lie he and Shannon had lived?

Fury held in submission for months now blazed through Jeremy's soul, and his hands shook. He had played the fool trying to please God. God could have stopped the savage killers, and Shannon would still be here with him. He and Shannon had honored God's plan and had waited to be together until they were married, but that hadn't been good enough. She was wrenched from his world, taken from all who loved her. And now he was alone and devastated.

Waves of raw agony, anger, and guilt flowed over Jeremy. His fists beat the ground until they throbbed. His body trembled with sobs, his rage no longer denied. "Why, God, why?" He buried his face in his hands and cried out. "Why did you take the only girl I ever loved? Why? I can't do this. Don't you know that? I did the right things," he shouted to the night sky, "I don't want to live without Shannon. I can't bear this agony." As he knelt there sobbing and exhausted with his head on his knees, a gentle breeze floated over him.

"Let go of the anger, Jeremy," a voice drifted through the wind. "It will tear you apart. God has a plan for you. Let go of the anger." The voice belonged to Shannon.

Stunned, Jeremy raised his head, half expecting to see Shannon's face before him. Had he been dreaming? The words replayed in his mind, "Let go of the anger. God has a plan for you." It was so like Shannon to say that. She was idealistic, always trusting God's plan. But how could this torture be a part of God's plan? He couldn't fathom anything good coming from Shannon's death. The only good thing in his life now was Heather. And even she was a reminder of his loss.

Jeremy struggled to his feet, remembering the reason for coming to this place of sorrow. "Pull yourself together," he scolded himself. The fierceness of the memories had taken him by surprise. He hadn't been prepared. That was why he was so emotional.

Still trembling, he wiped the dirt from his hands on his jeans and wheeled the stroller closer. He took Heather from the seat and sat down on the ground with her in his lap, facing the gravesite. "Shannon, I wanted to tell you that our baby was delivered after you died." His voice caught in his throat, and he waited until he could speak again. "Her name is—is Heather," he fought for the words, "Just like you wanted. She looks like you. Her hair is golden blond like yours." He swiped at the tears on his cheek. "It isn't easy, but we're making it. I just wanted you to know." His voice cracked, and he bit his lower lip. "I'm sorry I failed you." Father and child sat there in silence for several minutes; one lost in grief holding his only reason for living, the other aware only of her father's love.

Heather began to fuss, nudging Jeremy out of his deep

longing. He stood and caught sight of the rose with its now mangled stem lying on the ground. He lifted it to his lips, kissed the soft petals, and tenderly placed the broken rose on top of the grave marker, and whispered, "I love you, Shannon."

CHAPTER FIVE

Jeremy stared at the text. He had read the same page three times and didn't have a clue what it said. Concentration eluded him. Heather was sleeping peacefully, and he needed to take advantage of the time he had to study, but his mind drifted. More than a year had passed since Jeremy had returned to Cincinnati for the second semester of his junior year. His decision to return to school had more to do with needing something to focus on than a desire to continue his education. His loneliness for Shannon was still intense, but he'd become a master at stifling his anger and guilt. He had to move forward for both himself and his daughter. Friends helped him secure an apartment close to the campus, and he had found a nearby daycare that provided quality care to the children of students. He reconnected with classmates, and after a brief period of awkwardness, everything appeared to be back to normal.

Yet, it was not the same. Jeremy was the only one in his group of friends who had a child. He attended Bible study toting Heather along. She was popular with the students and always welcomed at their social gatherings. However, he no longer had the freedom to hang out all night and sleep late on the weekends. Heather was his first concern; he wanted her to be happy and well adjusted. Days filled with classes and a few hours of employment at the student library were his norm. Caring for Heather and studying made up his weekends. With financial help from his parents and a student loan, he could make ends meet, but there was not much money for extras. The life he once knew no longer existed.

Closing his book, he sighed. The Old Testament prophets would have to wait. It was useless to try to study any longer. Having no idea of what he had read, he decided to go to bed. He wandered into Heather's room, leaned over her crib, and gently ran a finger across her cheek. He stroked her blond curls, "You are my precious angel," he whispered and walked out the door. Though his life had changed, he couldn't imagine it without Heather. She was his life now.

* * *

Shannon's family gathered at Marianne and Frank's suburban house to celebrate Heather's third birthday. Heather's blond curls bounced as she laughed and ran around outside with her cousins. Her wavy blond hair was a gift from her mother, but the bright blue eyes and endearing smile were carbon copies of her father's.

The celebration was Jeremy's also. Though it had taken longer than he had planned, he graduated with honors and had already accepted a position as an associate minister with a growing church in the small town of Claymon about ten miles from his parent's house. He had also managed to acquire his first level EMT license, something he'd wanted since childhood. Shannon's family and his own were proud of his determination to finish college and be a good father.

Now, three years later, he had met both goals. Heather was a joyful, lively, and secure child.

Jeremy was helping his mother lode the dishwasher while the other adults visited in the living room. "It's a special day, Jeremy." Marianne's hand rested on Jeremy's shoulder as she slipped by him to clear dishes from the table. "We are so proud of you." She gave him a shaky smile.

"I could have never done it without you and Dad." He pulled her into a hug. "You guys are wonderful. You've supported me through all of this even though I disappointed you." His voice cracked. "I love you."

"You have never disappointed us. We are so proud of your perseverance and integrity."

Frank and Jessie walked into the kitchen, carrying dirty plates and cups. Frank looked at Jeremy, his eyes intense. "Your mother's right. Don't ever think you disappointed us, Son."

Jeremy's eyes grazed the floor. "At times I thought I wouldn't make it. I just wanted to give up." He raised his head. "But I couldn't. I didn't have that choice. There was always Heather to think about. Sometimes I wondered where God was—if He even knew me, or if I even cared anymore. But then, Heather would smile, or... or just need me. Then I knew I would make it." He stared at a point on the wall. "I know you all prayed for me. That's the only way I survived."

Heather pranced into the room, and Jeremy scooped her up, kissing her cheek. "Her birthdays are hard, though. I hate that Shannon's death will always cast a shadow on Heather's celebrations."

Jeremy's father's eyes fell on his granddaughter. "I know Heather's birthdays will always bring painful memories, but her life is the gift that makes it bearable. In time, the joy of watching Heather grow will soften your pain."

Jeremy and his family talked until late in the evening.

Jeremy shared his loneliness and grief over losing Shannon, his struggle to forgive himself for his inability to save her, and his doubts about the God he served. They listened, encouraged him, and assured him of God's love for him.

His fingers massaged his temples. "I hear you. I know you want me to believe that God has a plan. But if He truly loves me, why did he snatch Shannon away? What kind of plan is that?"

With concern in his blue eyes, Frank said. "We don't always understand God's way. It is just by faith that we know He loves us and wants what is best for us."

"But how could this be the best for me? Or Heather?" Jeremy said as he caught his sister's gaze for a second. He saw his doubt mirrored in her eyes before she turned away.

"I don't know all the reasons God lets us feel sorrow, Son. But I do know that He loves you. Someday you will feel joy again. I'm sure of it."

Jeremy doubted that statement. "I am doing all right, I guess. I have days that I can actually smile a little, but I'm not sure I will ever feel real joy again."

"You are a child of God, Jeremy." Marianne held his hand. "Remember, He does have a plan for you."

"For I know the plans I have for you," declares the Lord, "plans to prosper you, plans to give you hope and a future." (Jeremiah 29:11 NIV)

He knew the verse well. If only he could believe it.

CHAPTER SIX

Vikki checked her appearance in the mirror attached to her bedroom door for the umpteenth time. She lifted the ends of her shoulder-length brown hair with combs and then pulled them out again. The curling iron had only served to make her hair stick out in weird places. The polished, sophisticated look always eluded her. She tucked one side of her hair behind her ear and frowned at the mirror. It would have to do. She wanted to arrive a few minutes early to appear poised and self-assured, though she felt anything but confident.

She was encouraged, all the same, because this was her second interview with Claymon Elementary, situated in the town where she had recently moved. It was only a week before the school year started, leaving her anxious to find a teaching job. Filling out applications and waiting for phone calls took the majority of her summer. An invitation to a second interview made this prospect seem promising.

Vikki arrived at the Superintendent's Office with time to spare, hoping she would appear more composed than she felt as she ascended the few steps to the door. The interview went well, and her delight at an offer for a second-grade position overcame her natural inhibitions.

"Great, yes, thank you so much." She stood and then, to her embarrassment, noticed that the others were still seated. She sank into her chair, seeing the grins of those gathered at the table. "Sorry," she muttered as warmth crept up her cheeks.

Mrs. Richards, the principal of her school, smiled in return. "Welcome to the Claymon School System. I am sure you'll do a fine job for us. You can pick up information about our orientation day at the front desk. Your contract should be ready to sign by tomorrow afternoon if you want to stop in."

"That's fine." Vikki hesitated and glanced around the table.

"Thank you for coming, Miss Thompson. I'll see you in a few days." Mrs. Richards stood, signaling that the interview was over. Vikki thanked her again, retrieved the information from the front desk, and nearly skipped to her car.

Vikki drove the twenty minutes to her parents' house, hoping to find her mother there on her day off. As she turned into the well-kept older neighborhood where she had spent her childhood, she felt a little sorrowful that it was no longer hers. After her grandfather died ten years ago, her grandmother sold the land to a developer. She kept the two-story house, that now had cracks in some of its red bricks, and the five wooded acres it sat on. When her grandmother passed away last year, Vikki's parents inherited the property. They planned to keep the house for one of their daughters to rent and possibly purchase. Mary, her sister, was settled living close to the hospital where she was a nurse, so it seemed logical for Vikki to be the one to live there.

Wanting to keep the farmhouse in the family, Vikki had agreed to rent it and moved in last month. She liked the idea of living in her grandparents' home, but she was a bit nervous living alone. The possibility of finding a roommate was an idea she had been mulling over.

Another option was to rent out the small apartment on the second floor. Vikki's grandparents had taken in boarders occasionally, and though small, the apartment would be suitable for one person or a couple without children. That might be better, considering most of her close friends were either married or already settled in an apartment or house. By the time she reached her parents' house, she had decided to place an ad in the paper to rent the apartment.

* * *

Jeremy read, with interest, the ad describing the furnished apartment over a farmhouse in Claymon. It was worth checking out since the church he would be working in was located in that town. Jeremy had moved home until a place became available near his church and in his price range. His gig as the associate pastor wouldn't pay a lot, but he would do well enough since he had already found a part-time position as an EMT in Claymon. He tapped in the phone number and made an appointment to see the apartment the following afternoon.

Claymon was a growing town because of its proximity to a large urban community. Still, it maintained a small-town flavor because of an abundance of rural areas mixed in with the increase of restaurants, a grocery store, and a few retail businesses.

Jeremy consulted his GPS and made a right turn. As the farmhouse came into view, he smiled at the setting. Mature maple trees edged one side of the driveway shielding it from the housing development to the west. On the east side of the house, corn taller than Jeremy stood for acres with light brown tassels declaring harvest season was near. He drove up to the house and lifted Heather from her car seat. They walked down the cracked sidewalk and hopped up the two steps to the porch.

A young woman with light brown hair answered his ring. "Hi, I'm Vikki Thompson, and you must be Mr. Marcus." She smiled as she stood in the doorway.

"Yes, I'm Jeremy Marcus, and this is my daughter Heather." His eyes swept the property. "Lovely place you have here."

"Thank you." Vikki stepped aside. "Come in. We can get to the apartment from an inside staircase." She glanced at Heather as she climbed the stairs, "I hope I didn't mislead you. The apartment might be too small for your family," she said as she opened the door revealing the small living area.

"No, not at all. The ad stated that it had one bedroom. I was hoping I could purchase a sleeper sofa for myself." Jeremy's face lit up with understanding. "Oh, I forgot to mention that I'm a single parent. It's just Heather and me."

"Oh, I'm sorry." Her face flushed, and her green eyes grew round and wide. She brought her hands up to her necklace. "I mean… that's ok with me. I'm fine with that." Her voice rose higher. "The couch in the living room is a sleeper, anyway." She looked away, her cheeks rosy. "Go ahead and look around. I'll—I'll just wait here."

"I'll do that," Jeremy smiled, his eyes twinkling with amusement. Holding Heather by the hand, they walked through the door into the apartment. One room served as the kitchen and transitioned into an open space furnished with an oversized leather couch and two easy chairs. The sofa and chairs were an older style but in good shape. In the middle of the small kitchen stood a round table with four chairs. Everything was clean, and the appliances were in working order. A double bed and chest of drawers furnished the only bedroom.

Vikki cringed as she waited in the other room. *That's fine with me*; her words echoed in her head. She tried to settle herself as she heard Jeremy's approaching steps.

"I think this place will be fine. Heather can have the bedroom and the sleeper sofa will work for me. That is," Jeremy paused and tilted his head, his smile mischievous, "if you'll let a single parent move in."

"Of course," she stammered, her eyes shouting her unease. She tucked her hair behind her ear. "I... uh, when would you like to move in?"

"As soon as possible. Would this weekend be ok?" Jeremy slipped his hands into his front pockets.

"Sure, anytime. Come downstairs and I'll give you the key now." She paused, trying to regain some poise and sophistication. "This is for the door to your apartment," she explained and held out the key she plucked from a drawer by her refrigerator. "There is a staircase in the back of the house. We can walk there, so you can see the backyard." She led them around the house and waved her arm, indicating the apartment door. "There's your way in."

A portion of the large, shady yard was fenced. Jeremy climbed the stairway and gazed at the surroundings. "Is it a retriever?" he asked, pointing to a golden puppy.

"Yes, I just got her. She's a good companion." Vikki smiled at Heather. "You and Heather are welcome to play with her or go anywhere on the property for that matter."

Heather pulled on her father's hand. "I want to see the puppy. Please, Daddy."

"We might do that after we move in, ok?" Jeremy replied.

Heather's mouth made a pout. "I want to play with it now."

Jeremy bent down to her level. "Come on, Heather. We

will talk about playing with the puppy later. We need to go now. Say goodbye to Ms. Thompson."

Heather frowned but said, "Goodbye, Ms. uhm..."

"Bye, Heather. How about you call me Ms. Vikki?"

At that, the little girl smiled. "Bye, Ms. Vikki."

Jeremy smiled his goodbye and carefully descended the stairs holding Heather's hand. "Thank you, for the invitation to play in the yard with your puppy. We wouldn't want to bother your family, though."

"Oh, I live here alone. I'm single, too." Her voice sounded a little perkier than she expected. What was wrong with her? Why didn't she shout, *Hey, I think you're hot,* and be done with it.

If he noticed her embarrassment, it didn't show. "Well, I'll see you on Saturday then. Come on, Heather. Let's go tell Grandma and Grandpa what we found." He noticed the paper in his hand. "Oh, by the way, here is my list of references if you want to check me out." He took a quick breath and tossed her an embarrassed half-grin, "Uh, I mean check my references."

Vikki returned his awkward expression. "Oh, I guess I do need those."

"Yeah, feel free to call them if you want." He handed her the list, shook her hand, and walked to his car.

Vikki watched Jeremy's car until it turned onto the road. So much for being professional and self-assured, she thought with sarcasm. It was a stellar example of how to appear competent in a business transaction. She should give lessons.

Wandering over to the large front porch, she plopped down in the swing. The early August afternoon was typically hot, but the shaded yard provided some relief. Her thoughts drifted as she swung to and fro. This house had always held a special place in her heart, and now it offered her security. Her life was changing so quickly, and though moving here was part of that change, the farmhouse was an anchor, holding her steady, calming her. Adjusting to living alone, getting a new job, and renting the upstairs apartment were challenging tasks to her natural reserved nature. However, Vikki was pleased to have accomplished all of it by herself.

She felt blessed to have grown up in her family. It wasn't perfect, of course, but she had always felt loved and secure. She had been raised in a church, taught right from wrong, and got along well with her sister, Mary. Two years older and easily the prettiest girl in her class, Mary was confident and popular and Vikki's best friend.

The sound of car tires on the road shook her from her reverie. She stood up, stretched, looked out over her tree-filled front yard, and smiled. This lovely place was her home now. She couldn't imagine a better place.

* * *

Jeremy reclined against the back of the living room couch. A late-night news show spilled light in the darkness. His parents and sister had said their goodnights an hour ago; he was alone with his thoughts. Three years ago, he had been a mortally wounded man; now, he was a man saved by the love of a child. Two thousand years ago, a child was born, restoring mortally wounded humankind. He marveled at the parallel.

Heather was indeed a redeemer in his life, a beacon when darkness threatened to suffocate him. When depression sought to wring the very life from Jeremy, Heather had been the glimmer of hope, enabling him to claw through the darkness, struggle for breath, and rekindle his will to live again. Through Heather, God had begun healing Jeremy's soul and now brought him to this crossroad. Jeremy told himself he would never forget his love for Shannon, but he must attempt to move on, knowing he would never love in that way again.

Yet, despite his revival from the darkness of depression, regardless of his determination, somewhere deep within the walls surrounding his heart, fear and anger lurked, ever ready to purge any happiness that threatened to penetrate the fortress.

Jeremy had accepted his role of being a single parent; he loved Heather with his whole being, but if God did have a plan for him, other than his ministry and going through the motions of living, he couldn't imagine it. He knew he shouldn't doubt God's wisdom and love, but the questions remained unresolved. What bothered him most was that Shannon's horrible death, leaving him to raise a child alone, could be part of a plan to prosper him and give him a future. Shannon had been his future. Would real happiness ever be a part of his life again?

CHAPTER SEVEN

Jessie rolled over and stretched her arms over her head, longing to stay beneath the covers, but she couldn't this morning because she promised Jeremy. She did want to hear Jeremy's first sermon as the associate pastor of New Life Community Church. Even though she had abandoned the practice of attending church every week, she was proud of her brother and his faith.

It wasn't that she didn't believe in God, but she didn't buy into the whole Christian bureaucracy anymore. She loved and respected her father, and she attended church with her family about once a month, primarily for his benefit. However, she could only support her father's church on a fundamental level because of its position on specific issues, especially women's role in the church. The culture had dictated women's role in the early church when they were uneducated and seen merely as property. Why couldn't people understand that it was different now? Many practices followed in biblical times were no longer valid. Countless discussions had occurred between Jessie and her father, and because of deep mutual respect, they chose to agree to disagree on several matters.

Jessie did believe, though, and her issues were with certain types of Christians and not with God. She had seen hypocrisy and self-righteous attitudes among Christians within the church. Undeniably, she did have more liberal views than most of her fellow church members on issues, such as evolution, politics, and the persistence of outdated traditions, and they certainly had a right to disagree with her opinions. It was the way they disagreed that frustrated her.

She would never forget the rejection she'd felt as a senior in high school when she had dared voice her opinion about evolution. She hadn't been arguing for the theory of evolution; she just asserted that it was essential to examine.

"Oh my goodness, Jessie," her teacher, Mr. Matthews, exclaimed with an astonished and condescending gaze, "You surely don't believe in evolution. You're the preacher's daughter after all. Why, what would your father say?"

"I don't know. Why don't you ask him?" Jessie shot back, her amber eyes flashing. Mr. Matthews stared at her with crossed arms. "I really don't think we need to discuss this any further. It has no relevance for this class."

"If you can't even entertain a discussion on the matter, then you must not have much faith in your position."

Mr. Matthews glared at her. "I think I need to speak to your father, young lady. You are insolent and disrespectful."

Jessie lifted her chin. "He's in the building."

Several of her classmates stared at Jessie as if she had committed blasphemy. All she had asked was how Christians could ignore the possibility that the theory of evolution might have some scientific merit. She had wanted a discussion, not a scolding.

Mr. Matthews strode up to Jessie's father after Sunday School. "I'd like a word with you, Pastor."

"Of course," Pastor Marcus replied. "How can I help you?"

"Your daughter was quite rude to me in class today," Mr. Matthews asserted.

"Oh...," he looked at his daughter with raised eyebrows, "that surprises me. I've never known Jessie to be disrespectful to her teachers."

Mr. Matthews scowled at her. "Well, she was today," he insisted and recounted the incident that had occurred in class.

Sixteen-year-old Jeremy stifled a grin and winked at his sister. Frank locked eyes with Jessie for a second, turned back to her teacher, and then responded in a way she would never forget. "Mr. Matthews, it seems to me that Jessie had a legitimate point, and while I may not agree with it, I do believe she has the right to express it. She is an intelligent girl, and I trust that being my daughter doesn't preclude her from stating her own beliefs." He glanced at Jessie, who was staring at him with a gaping mouth. "I will, however, speak to her about the need to always treat people, especially her teachers, with respect even when she disagrees with them."

"Well, I certainly hope you do. You also might give her a refresher course on church doctrine," Mr. Matthews said with a huff and stormed off.

Jeremy grinned at the retreating teacher, shook his finger, and pretended to stomp away in a rare show of impudence. Catching his antics out of the corner of his eye, his father tossed him a withering look that stopped Jeremy in his tracks.

Jessie thanked her father for his support and admitted she had been a little sarcastic. He put his hands on her shoulders and met her gaze. "Jessie, I will always defend you as long as you are honorable in your beliefs. I don't think God wants you to blindly follow everything you hear in church, even from me. Read the Bible for yourself and be clear about what

you believe, and please," he gave a small smile, glancing in
Mr. Matthew's direction, "be respectful when you disagree."

"As for you, young man...," he turned to face Jeremy.

"Gotta go find Mom," Jeremy interrupted and darted off.

Jessie was grateful for her father's resolve to let her think
independently. However, she knew he was troubled by her
lack of enthusiasm for church and her continual questioning
of traditions and rituals. She would never think of intention-
ally hurting or disappointing him, so she kept many of her
comments to herself.

Coming back to the present, Jessie hurried to get her
shower. It wouldn't be good to be late for Jeremy's first
sermon at his new church.

* * *

New Life Community Church had welcomed Jeremy and
Heather with pleasure. The charismatic and sincere young
minister had alleviated any reservations about a single father
taking a leadership position. The way he cared for Heather
made him all the more endearing.

Jeremy was ready early, having allowed more than
enough time to get both Heather and himself prepared for
this morning. His intended message was down-to-earth, on
the subject of God's grace in times of failure, and he already
felt comfortable with the people. Nonetheless, he felt a little
anxious about preaching in front of his family, who planned
to attend his first sermon. He had been a guest speaker at his
father's church on several occasions, but this was different.
This was his church.

He hoped his fiercely independent sister would feel
comfortable at New Life Community and maybe even decide
to attend on occasion. Her major conflict with their father's
church would be of no consequence here. New Life was

smaller and relaxed enough that they used anyone willing to help, regardless of gender. Several women taught adult Sunday school classes that included both men and women. He knew his father's church didn't approve of women teaching men, but he suspected it was more tradition than doctrine.

Jeremy had always had a special place in his heart for his sister. At 5'9", Jessie was only an inch shorter than Jeremy and had the same engaging smile. Wavy, chin-length, dark brown hair framed her face, giving her a striking look.

Jeremy was two years younger than Jessie, and they had always been close despite the differences in their personalities. Jessie's nature was independent, daring, and intense. Yet underneath her bold exterior, she was loyal, compassionate, and even a tad insecure. Often opinionated, and while not obstinate in her beliefs, she gladly shared her views. Though she claimed to dislike useless traditions, her love for her family, especially Jeremy, was indisputable.

It was time to leave. As he backed down the driveway, he saw Vikki come out of her front door. She smiled and waved. He returned her wave and, for some reason, recalled the deep green color of her eyes.

CHAPTER EIGHT

Vikki walked into the First United Methodist Church, found her family, and sat down with them.

"Hi, dear. How are you? How are things going with your new renter?" Her mother whispered.

"Oh, fine. He's really friendly." She looked down the pew at Mary and her boyfriend. Robbie had his arm draped over the back of the bench with his hand resting on Mary's shoulder. Mary caught her eye and smiled. Why wouldn't she be happy? Robbie was ruggedly handsome with blond hair and blue eyes. On top of that, he was here at church making points with her parents. Mary was lucky to find a guy like him.

The organ began to play, and the congregation sang the opening songs. Vikki tried to be attentive to the message, but her thoughts drifted over the last month. Four weeks into the school year, she was adjusting well to teaching. An attack of nerves had made her stomach churn her first morning while waiting for her students to arrive.

She had made name tags, planned a get-acquainted activity, and asked the teacher across the hall, Lisa, a thousand questions, yet still felt insecure about how to begin teaching.

"You will be fine," the seasoned teacher said. "I remember my first day. I was nearly sick with worry. It's natural to feel nervous at first." She smiled with compassion. "If you need anything, I'll be right across the hall."

Vikki had made it through the day just as Lisa had predicted, and it hadn't been that bad. Each day she gained more confidence, and though a few of the students had behavior issues, most of them were well behaved and enjoyable to teach. She fit in well with the other teachers and had become close to Lisa, who had taught for fifteen years, a lifetime in Vikki's mind.

"I don't know if I will last fifteen years."

"That's what I thought," Lisa informed her with a grin. "I couldn't imagine teaching for even ten years, yet here I am. It is amazing how the years slip away."

Then there was her tenant. Appearing at her door three Saturdays ago with a man she assumed to be his father and a lovely brunette, he announced, "I just wanted to let you know that we're here. We'll go ahead and get started if it's still okay with you that I move in," he said with a teasing smile.

She blushed but met his eyes. "Of course, Mr. Marcus, let me know if you need anything, I'll be here for a while."

"Okay, but please call me Jeremy." He paused and addressed the man with him. "We better start moving things in. It shouldn't take too long since we don't have any furniture to worry about." Vikki watched the three of them walk to the car. The young woman was probably his girlfriend. She hoped not, surprising herself that she cared.

A couple of hours later, Vikki decided to drive over to Claymon Elementary to finish up a bulletin board. She walked out the door, considering whether to tell Jeremy that she was leaving when he rounded the corner of the house with his arm around the brunette. So, she was his girlfriend.

"We're finished here for now," he stated. "Heather and I will be back this evening."

"Okay, I'll be here later if you need anything."

He slipped his hands in his pockets and smiled at her. "Well, I guess I'll see you later then."

As it turned out, Vikki didn't see her Jeremy either Sunday or Monday. His car was gone Sunday morning when she left for church, but it was parked in the driveway when she returned. Maybe he picked up that girl that helped him move in and brought her here. They were probably sharing dinner in his new apartment. She chided herself for caring about Jeremy and his girlfriend. If things had turned out differently in her relationship with Tom, if she had been prettier or more outgoing, she would be sharing her lunch with someone, too.

Early Tuesday evening, Vikki pulled up to her garage just as Jeremy was getting out of his car. It had been a tiring day, and she had several sets of papers to grade. Jeremy approached her car door. "Long day?"

"Very. How about yours?" She pulled out a bag of papers and several books from the car.

"Not too bad, I was putting in a few hours at the fire station." Observing her heavy load, he came closer. "Here, let me carry something."

"Thanks, I'm too tired to make another trip," she agreed, handing him the books.

They walked in silence to the porch with Heather prancing ahead. As they approached the door, Vikki reached for the books. "Thank you for your help. I think I can manage now." On an impulse, she looked up at Jeremy. "Would you like to come in for a glass of tea?"

"Actually, I was wondering if you would care to join us for

hamburgers on the grill. I have plenty and would like the company." He looked as if his words surprised him.

"Okay, sure, if it's no bother," Vikki said with eyes wide.

"It's no bother at all." He took Heather's hand. "As I said, I would enjoy the company. Heather is a great companion but not the best conversationalist. Come on up as soon as you're ready. I'll go ahead and start the grill."

Vikki changed into jeans and a t-shirt, scowled at her reflection in the mirror, and hurried to the kitchen. She rummaged through the cabinets, found some corn chips, and headed for the steps to Jeremy's balcony.

The aroma drifting through the air made Vikki realize how hungry she was as she climbed the steps. She went in through the open gate, "Hi, I brought some chips." She placed the bag on the table.

"Thanks, the burgers will be ready in a few minutes. Have a seat while I go get our drinks."

It was a pleasantly warm evening. A slight breeze played in the trees, rippling gently through Vikki's hair as they sat on the balcony. She hadn't expected to feel so comfortable with Jeremy, but he was easy to talk to and genuinely inter-ested in her job as a teacher, asking about her first day and declaring that he wouldn't know what to do with a classroom full of kids. Their conversation was easy as they ate.

"You seem to do great with Heather," Vikki spoke her thoughts without meaning to. "I mean, it must be difficult raising a child on your own," she stammered, her face flushing.

"Thanks, it's more lonely than difficult I guess." He smiled faintly. "I don't really have a lot of time for a social life."

"But I bet your girlfriend adores Heather," she dared.

"Girlfriend?" He said with a confused look.

"Oh," she hesitated. "Well, I thought—I mean the—the girl who helped you move in..." Her voice fell, and her fingers twisted the gold cross on her necklace. Her eyes studied the ground.

Jeremy's tone held a tinge of surprise, "That was my sister, Jessie. I don't have a girlfriend."

"Oh." Vikki lifted her head and met his eyes.

An awkward silence settled between them. Jeremy was the first to speak. "I guess I haven't really told you much about me."

"No, I guess you haven't."

"What would you like to know?"

"You... you don't have to tell me anything. I didn't mean to pry." She rose from her chair feeling foolish. "I probably ought to be going anyway. Thanks for dinner."

"Hey, wait." He touched her arm. "Don't leave, we haven't had our ice cream yet." He ran his hand through his dark blond hair and smiled, "Please stay."

She lowered herself in the chair. "Well, I guess I could stay for a little while longer, especially if there's ice cream."

Vikki relaxed as they ate ice cream and watched Heather play with her dolls. She kept bringing her "baby" to Jeremy and having him babysit while she pretended to go to the doctor. Vikki joined the game, and the three of them played house until Heather lost interest in the game and left to play with her blocks.

Jeremy laughed. "You know you will have to come again. Heather has found a new playmate." He folded his arms on the table, "I didn't tell you I was a minister, did I?"

"No," Vikki answered, her eyes wide. "I guess I thought you were a fireman." He didn't look a bit like a preacher clad in his faded jeans and t-shirt.

"I do have my EMT license, and I'm working part-time at the Claymon Fire Station, but my full-time job is associate pastor at New Life Community Church."

Vikki nodded, "I just moved here a few months ago. Is it the one on Vine Street?"

"Yes, that's the one. Maybe you could visit sometime. Where do you go to church?" She noticed he asked where she went, not if she went. "I go to a Methodist church in Indianapolis with my parents."

"Oh, that's nice." He paused, and scooped up another bite, "But if you ever want to visit New Life, we'd love to have you."

"Okay, I'll keep that in mind."

Vikki finished her ice cream while they chatted then declared she needed to get busy grading her papers. He agreed saying it was time to get Heather to bed.

She said goodbye and left through his balcony door. She'd had an enjoyable time, but now she would have to pay for it by staying up late preparing her plans for tomorrow.

She talked with Jeremy frequently over the next few days, growing more comfortable around him with each encounter. So, when he suggested she go with Heather and him for pizza on Friday, she readily agreed. After Vikki mentioned that she liked playing cards, Jeremy suggested that she come up to his apartment when they got home for a couple of games of Rummy. They played until midnight, and then Vikki insisted that she needed to get home, or she wouldn't be able to wake up in time to go shopping with her mother in the morning.

"Well, all right, we couldn't have you being a grumpy shopper. Your mother might think you were out all night with some good-looking guy."

"Oh, don't worry. I'll tell her that it was just you," Vikki teased, and immediately felt warmth creeping up her cheeks.

"Ouch," he said, a smile spreading across his face. Rising from his chair, he picked up a towel and playfully swatted Vikki's arm.

Her hand tipped over her glass as she jumped up, spilling her drink on the table. "Oh, I'm so sorry!" she exclaimed, grabbing the towel.

Jeremy laughed and snatched the towel from her. "It was my fault, don't worry." He wet the cloth and wiped the table. Then he swatted her again. "But..., you did start it."

"What did I do?" She tilted her head, and her green eyes sparkled as she attempted an innocent appearance. Jeremy caught his breath. He stood very close, gazing in her eyes for several seconds.

"Your eyes look really green tonight, almost an emerald color," he breathed. He dipped his head a bit but caught himself and pulled back, still caught in her gaze.

Vikki tore her eyes away, "Well, I better go now." She fiddled with her necklace. "I'll use the stairs that lead from your apartment to my kitchen."

After a beat, Jeremy found his voice. "Sure, that way you won't have to walk outside." He led her to the door and opened it. "Goodnight, have fun with your mom tomorrow."

"Thanks, I will." She noticed him watching her walk down the stairs. When she reached the bottom, she looked up at him and waved, "Night."

"Night." Jeremy pulled the door closed.

Vikki chatted briefly with Jeremy on Saturday when she returned home, but he seemed different, distant somehow. Maybe she had misread his actions the night before, though she had been sure he had almost kissed her. Who was she kidding? A guy like Jeremy would never be interested in her. Every young single woman at New Life Community would have her eyes on him. His worries of a sparse social life would soon be over, with all the flirtations he was sure to receive from women eager to capture his interest. Perhaps he would still find a little time to play cards or go out for pizza with her, but she doubted it would be very often.

Her mother's voice brought her out of her daydream. "Are you going to stand for the prayer?" she whispered.

"Oh, sorry." She jumped up and bowed her head.

Outside in the parking lot, her sister eyed her. "You obviously had something on your mind more interesting than the sermon," she teased, her large brown eyes curious. "Whoever it was must be awfully good-looking."

"I was just thinking about school." It was at least partially true.

"Right." Mary rolled her eyes. "See you at Mom and Dad's."

Robbie smiled at her. "Maybe it's some handsome teacher at work."

Vikki had to laugh as she thought of the prospects at her school.

CHAPTER NINE

The morning had gone well, and Jeremy received several compliments on his message. Of course, his family thought it was excellent, but he also received praise from others. Brandon Winters, the senior pastor, and his wife Alice insisted that he and Heather join them for dinner at their home after the service. Brandon was in his mid-fifties with salt and pepper hair and a boyish grin that made him appear younger than his years. His wife, a petite blond, complimented her husband's quiet nature with her bubbly personality.

Late that afternoon, Jeremy thanked his hosts for lunch and said his goodbyes.

"You are always welcome here," Alice replied. "I think you are going to be a real asset to the church. You will appeal to the younger crowd, as well as the older members. Now all we need to do is find you a good woman." She crossed her arms and beamed as if she were the first person to ever come up with such a grand idea.

Jeremy cringed inside. Why were church people always so

troubled about his single status? Everywhere he interviewed, the leadership had questioned him about getting married again, hinting that searching for a wife should be his top priority. Nothing could be further from his mind. He always gave some evasive answer about God's will, hoping it would curtail additional questions. Church leadership seemed keen on their preacher being married—especially if he had a child.

"I'm doing just fine, thanks," he said with measured tones.

"Oh, now," she said with a wave. "I can introduce you to several lovely ladies from church."

He half smiled, inching toward the door. "Thanks again for the dinner. I'll see you next Sunday."

On the drive home, his thoughts turned to Shannon. Three years after her death, memories of her were no longer an ongoing source of pain that overshadowed his life. Most of the time, they resided in the distant corridors of his heart. Periods of dark, desperate grief and frightful dreams of that terrible night still accosted him in moments of weakness. Still, the episodes had become less frequent over time. And when his feelings of anger toward God threatened to arise, he shoved them ever deeper into the dark spaces in his spirit. He had even learned to smile again and being a father to Heather brought him contentment. Yet, dark memories and guilt skulked below the surface, always ready to haunt him when summoned.

Alice's words had beckoned them this time, and they threatened to engulf him.

The pastor's wife seemed certain Jeremy needed to find a wife and mother for Heather. Maybe she was right. Possibly, Heather did need a mother. Both of her grandmothers and Aunt Jessie were a part of her life. But was that enough? It would have to be because he would never know the kind of love he'd had with Shannon again.

"Oh, God, why did you take Shannon from me?" he asked aloud.

The sound of his voice startled him, and he looked in the rearview mirror to see Heather's reaction, but she was sleeping peacefully. He sighed and closed his mind to the darkness. He must be strong for Heather.

He turned on some music, determined to put an end to this line of thought. An image of Vikki with her emerald green eyes came to his mind. *What was that about? Why did I think of her?* He cranked up the volume on the radio.

* * *

"Hey, Preacher, you with me?" The dark-haired paramedic paused in his instruction of procedures to follow with burn victims. "You look like you're a thousand miles away." The two other EMTs smirked. Jordan, Jeremy's mentor at the fire station, was fun-loving and slightly irreverent, often joking around with his co-workers. Jeremy had noticed, though, the rescue workers admired Jordan for his integrity and professionalism, and Jordan showed great compassion for those who required his professional skills.

"Sorry, Jordan. I was just drifting, I guess."

"Obviously, it's time for class to be over." he grinned and looked at his three students. "You guys are dismissed."

"See ya, Jordan," said one of the men as they walked away.

Jeremy approached Jordan as he was gathering his supplies. "Hey, I am sorry. You have a lot of good information, and I do listen to you."

"No problem. It's time for lunch anyway." Jordan gave a slight shrug. "I could use some company. Pizza okay with you?"

"Sure," Jeremy replied, "and thanks for being patient with me."

. . .

Jordan grinned playfully across the restaurant table, "So, were you dreaming about some cute chick from that church of yours during my lecture this morning?"

"Hardly," Jeremy smiled faintly, "I've just been dealing with memories a little, I guess."

"Well, you've been through a lot." Jordan's look was direct. Jeremy had told him only that Shannon died in childbirth, but Jordan had sensed by the pain in Jeremy's eyes that there was more to the story than his new friend was ready to share.

"But, I also have a lot to be thankful for: Heather, my parents, and my church family." He paused and looked at Jordan. "You really should visit New Life Community Church, you know."

"Well, I just might. I can't seem to find a church that will put up with me, though," he kidded. "Actually, I would like to find one close by. Are there any good-looking girls there?"

Jeremy rolled his eyes. "I try not to look. The pastor's wife is determined to marry me off."

Jordan's brown eyes flickered with fun, betraying his solemn tone. "Maybe you'd better look, or who knows what you'll end up with." His smile turned mischievous, "Maybe I *should* come, you know, just to help you look."

Jeremy laughed. "Do come, and look for yourself, but I'm not interested."

Jordan's expression turned thoughtful. "You know you might want to remarry someday, for Heather's sake as well as yours."

Exasperation shadowed Jeremy's eyes. "Not you too," he said, "I know Heather needs a mother, but I just don't see that ever happening."

"Sorry, it's none of my business. I'm sure you don't need my advice. Are you ready to go?"

"Yes, but you can give me advice anytime. I enjoy your candor."

CHAPTER TEN

A t 5:30 in the evening, the only other person in the building was the custodian. "Do you mind if I go ahead and sweep the floor, Miss Thompson?"

"Not at all, I'm almost ready to go," Vikki answered, smiling up at her from her desk.

The custodian leaned on her vacuum. "Do you have a big weekend planned?"

"No, not really. Do you?"

"My grandson is coming to visit from Michigan," she beamed. "I haven't seen him for almost six months."

"I'm sure you're excited then." Vikki smiled at the older woman. "How old is he?"

"He's three."

"That's a fun age, isn't it?"

"Yes, it is. Well, I'll let you get back to work." She finished sweeping and waved her hand, "Don't stay too late. A pretty girl like you surely has something better to do on a Friday night."

"I won't stay long, I'm almost finished here." It didn't

matter because the custodian was wrong. She didn't have anything better to do.

On her drive home, Vikki thought about Heather. She wondered if she was getting too close to the little girl. She had seen Jeremy and his daughter in the backyard the day before playing with Clover. Heather had hurried over to the fence and reached for Vikki. Jeremy ambled over to her. "She really likes you. Why don't you come join us?" All three of them played ball with Clover, and when the puppy grew tired, Vikki and Jeremy talked about their day and watched Heather play with her dolls.

An hour later, Vikki glanced at her phone. "I need to go and get some work done."

"Don't go yet," Heather pouted and clung to Vikki. Vikki knelt so she was at Heather's eye level, "Honey, I have to go, but I'll come visit again." She felt Jeremy's eyes on her as she hugged Heather goodbye. She stood and faced him. "See you later."

"Sure, come any time." His eyes had held hers for a moment before he looked away.

Vikki remembered, now, how Jeremy had looked at her yesterday. Maybe he was attracted to her. No, that couldn't be. He was trying to be friendly. He was lonely and appreciated having someone to talk to; that was all.

By the time she reached the old farmhouse driveway, she had decided to ask Jeremy and Heather over for supper if they didn't have other plans. Her plans were sparse this weekend, and she didn't want to sit at home alone. She wanted company. Jeremy's car was in his parking place. Good, maybe he didn't have plans. Leaving her bags in the car, she marched up the stairs outside his apartment before she could change her mind. She knocked and fiddled with the cross around her neck while she waited.

"Hi there." He didn't seem at all displeased to see her.

"I—I—would you like to come over?" she blurted, sounding like a young schoolgirl.

Jeremy's eyebrows arched in amusement. "To play?"

She squeezed her lips together. "For pizza. I thought we could have one delivered."

"Sure," he winked, "we'll be right down."

Her cheeks grew warm, "You can just come down your kitchen stairs when you're ready; my door is unlocked."

It promised to be a good evening. The uncomfortable feeling had faded, and Jeremy was relaxed and friendly. They ate, then talked and played with Heather until Jeremy noticed it was her bedtime. "Why don't you come up to my place for a few hands of Rummy after I get Heather to bed?" he suggested.

"That sounds fun, if you're sure it's not too late."

"It's only 9:30, I think I can handle a couple of hours yet," he joked. "Give me about thirty minutes to get Heather down, and I will call you."

"Okay then, prepare to be trounced."

His eyes sparkled. "You're dead meat, Babe." He looked slightly puzzled for a second, then said, "See you, soon."

* * *

They played three games, and Vikki won two of them. "I really should be going," she yawned. "I've been up late grading papers all week."

"Aw, it's early yet. Let's sit outside for a little bit. There won't be very many nice nights left before winter."

Vikki followed him out to the balcony. The night sky was beautiful, clear, and starlit, with a slight breeze stirring the air. She stood looking out over the rail. "I love fall. It's my favorite season when the days are still warm and the nights are cool and starry like they are tonight."

Jeremy stood beside her with memories of another starry night threatening to overtake the moment. No, he wouldn't think of that night. All he wanted now was to stand here with Vikki and enjoy her company.

"You're awfully quiet." She looked up at him and tucked her hair behind her ear. "Do you want to go back in?"

"No, I want to be right here with you." Even as he spoke, a loud inner voice pierced his heart. *Remember Shannon, she's the only woman you'll ever want.* A shadowy image of Shannon's face with her golden hair shimmered on the horizon of his mind, just beyond his reach. He gazed at the woman in front of him. She was lovely, tangible, and alive. Shannon's face floated into focus, then blurred and drifted away.

Jeremy inched closer to Vikki. His blue eyes were intense.

He ran a gentle finger across her cheek and down her jawline. He dipped his head, and his lips grazed hers, surrendering to the battle raging in his heart. Lost in the moment, he kissed her again.

"*Traitor, cheater,*" breathed his desperate accuser. He backed away, drawing a deep breath. "I'm sorry," his voice cracked, "I can't. I can't do this." His features crumbled, and he dropped his hands.

Vikki stared at him. "What's wrong?" She stepped back, wrapped her arms around herself, and shivered.

Fighting for control, he took her hands in his and searched for words. "I'm sorry. That should have never happened," he breathed in deeply. "I—I didn't mean to upset you."

"Upset me?" Her arms stiffened by her side. "What do you mean?" Her expression was cold. "You do have a girlfriend, don't you?"

He shook his head, "No I don't, it's not that, but..." he eyed the ground. "Maybe we should just be friends."

"Just friends?" She tossed her head and jerked her hands away from his. "Yeah, I know what that means. The next line is, 'You're too good for me.'" Her voice shook. "What that really means is I'm just not your type, right? I'm not pretty enough, not desirable enough!" She hesitated for a moment then spat out the rest, "Not *good* enough for you!" She whirled away from him and flew down the outside steps of the balcony with reckless speed.

"Stop, you're going to fall!" Jeremy cried out. Running after her, he caught her by the arm and righted her as she stumbled on the bottom step. "What's wrong with you? Please calm down."

Vikki lifted her chin. "Please let go of me, I want to go home," she demanded. Her words were like ice as she tugged at her hands and turned her face away.

He held her hands more firmly and swung her around to face him. Bewilderment emanated from his eyes. "Listen to me for a minute."

She raised her head to the sky. "I don't have to listen to you."

He stared at her, stunned by her boldness. "Okay, don't listen, but I'm going to tell you anyway." His expression softened. "Please come back up and let me explain."

"You can explain right here."

"Please, come back up to the balcony. I need to be able to hear Heather if she wakes up."

Vikki marched up the steps, plopped down at the table. "I'm listening."

Jeremy walked to the table, positioned himself in a chair directly in front of her, and rubbed his temples. "First of all, I don't have a girlfriend. I'm just not ready for... I—I'm not over Heather's mother." His eyes were deep pools of sorrow.

Vikki's voice came down a notch. "What happened to her?"

He fixed his gaze on the floor. "She... she died."

Vikki drew her breath in sharply and stared at her lap. "I'm so sorry. I didn't know. I just thought..."

He took her hands. "You had no way of knowing." He raised her chin and searched her face. "Look at me." He marveled at her self-assessment. "I don't know where you got the idea that you're not pretty, cause you're wrong. I think you're lovely." He gave a little shrug, "That's the trouble."

Vikki tilted her head to one side, "What do you mean?"

Jeremy gazed at her with his mouth open. She wasn't aware of the effect she had on him. He gave her hands a gentle squeeze. "Vikki, don't you see? I'm attracted to you—a lot. I—," he struggled for words. "Kissing you was awesome, but I—I thought about Shannon and...," his voice failed.

Vikki drew her hands from Jeremy's and rubbed her fingers together. "It's guilt? You feel guilty for kissing me?" She looked away for a moment, then turned and studied his sorrowful face. "I'm sorry," she whispered, "I don't know what to say." She twisted her necklace with closed eyes. "I should go now."

"No, I'm the one who should be sorry. I'm not trying to play games with you." He shifted in his chair. "Look at me. Please."

She did as he asked and laid her hands on the table. "Shannon must have been very special to you. Do you want to talk about it?"

Jeremy was surprised, but not put off, by her question. "She was special," he said. His eyes filled, and he blinked in vain at the tears. "She was murdered." He paused, "Abused and murdered while I was beaten and then stabbed." He bit his lower lip, took a ragged breath, and waited until he was able to speak again. "Heather was delivered by paramedics after Shannon died. They saved our baby, but they couldn't save her." He rose, walked to the balcony fence, gripped the top rail, and stared out into the darkness. "I'm just trying to learn to live with it." A tear trickled down his cheek, but he didn't brush it away. Why was the pain still so fresh and agonizing?

Vikki waited a minute, then walked to his side. "I'm sorry."

Jeremy turned to face her and took her hands. A tear dropped on his fingers; He didn't know if it fell from his eyes or Vikki's.

They stood there for several minutes until Jeremy broke the silence. "Let's sit down, and I'll tell you the whole story."

"You don't have to if it's too painful."

"I want you to know. I haven't told anyone all the details, not even my family. But I feel I need to tell you." He stopped and met her eyes. "That is—if you want to know."

"Of course, but only if you're sure."

"I am."

Jeremy told her everything he remembered about that fateful night. Although it wounded him gravely, it peeled off a layer of heaviness in his soul to relate the atrocities he'd found too terrible to speak of since the night of Shannon's death. The horrifying details left Vikki wide-eyed, yet she listened to the whole story.

"She was terrified and alone. I couldn't save her," Jeremy finished and buried his face in his hands. He sat without moving in the stillness of the night.

Vikki shifted in her chair. "Thank you for sharing your story with me. I remember hearing about that incident, but I didn't remember any names of the people. I know it was painful for you to talk about it. I can't imagine anything so terrible." She angled her head. "You know it wasn't your fault, though, right? No one could have saved her."

He stood up and looked deeply into her green eyes. "Thank you for listening. I guess I've needed to tell the whole story to someone. I hope it didn't upset you too much."

"No, I feel honored that you trusted me with your story." She hugged him, and Jeremy felt her warmth waft over his body and drain his sadness.

At last, Vikki released her hug. "It's late. I should probably go now."

They walked through the kitchen to her door, and facing her, he touched her arm.

"Thank you for listening." He pulled her to him again, needing her closeness, and brushed his lips on her cheek.

Vikki stepped back, looked at him with those green eyes, and curved her lips in a sad smile. "I'll see you later." She opened the door and walked down the stairs, leaving Jeremy to still his racing heart.

* * *

The dragon-like demon tore into Jeremy and jerked his legs around like he was a rag doll. With ferocious strength, it yanked him into the abyss—away from Shannon, whose outstretched arms pleaded for deliverance. Jeremy clung to the rim of the dark pit, his fingers clawing the dirt, fighting in desperation to keep his head from sinking below the earth. Shannon needed him. She disappeared from his vision as the demon dragged him further into the pit. Her shrieks ripped through him like a searing blade.

"Let go of me," Jeremy screamed with fury, his feet thrashing in every direction in a vain attempt to dislodge his assailant. The dragon's evil laughter rose higher. Flames spewed from its mouth as its grip chewed into Jeremy's legs, heaving him ever deeper into the pit of blackness. "I'm coming, Shannon. I'm coming. Oh, God, help me. Help me!"

Jeremy bolted upright in bed at the chilling sound of a scream. Racing to Heather's room, he found her asleep. A wave of nausea and dizziness drove him to the floor. The scream had been his own.

CHAPTER ELEVEN

Jeremy spent Saturday morning at the fire station. Even though sleep had eluded him for several hours, he was determined to put the events of the night before to rest for now. He and Jordan made two accident runs, both with only minor injuries. They stopped at the local pizza joint for a quick lunch on the way back from the second run.

"You're doing a good job, you know," Jordan said between bites of pizza.

Jeremy shook his head. "I don't know. I haven't had to face really tough circumstances yet. I'm not sure how I'll respond if someone doesn't make it."

"Luckily, we don't have to deal with those types of situations around here too much." His look was steady. "But when you are faced with a critical situation, I'm sure you'll be able to handle it."

"What makes you so sure?"

Jordan grinned, "Because, Preacher Boy, I've seen you in action. You catch on fast, you're quick to react in an emergency, and you're sensitive to the needs of others. I'd ride with you anytime."

Jeremy appreciated the praise from his skilled and respected mentor. But Jeremy knew Jordan wasn't aware that he had already been faced with a deadly situation and had been powerless against it. "Thanks, I appreciate your faith in me. I hope you're right."

"So, what are you doing this afternoon? You're welcome to hang around the station. I could use the help."

"Thanks, but I need to get Heather from Mom's and then pick up a few groceries. Have you given any more thought about visiting New Life Community? I'm not preaching tomorrow, just reading scripture and leading the opening prayer, but I'd love for you to come."

Jordan shrugged, "Why not? I'd like to find a place a little closer. What time is the service?"

Jeremy gave him the information, and they headed out to the rescue truck. Jordan nudged him in the arm. "Has the preacher's wife set you up with any pretty women yet?" he teased.

"No, fortunately, but I'm sure she hasn't given up the idea," he muttered.

Jordan laughed. "Oh, you poor boy. We all have problems, don't we?"

They drove the distance to the station in companionable silence. Jeremy let his thoughts return to last evening. After Shannon died, he had bolted the door to his heart and had never considered unlocking it. It wasn't a conscious choice; being alone was just something Jeremy had accepted without considering any other option. And until a few weeks ago, he had no reason to believe that anyone would cause his heart to push against the securely locked door. Sharing his story with Vikki was good, though. It would help her understand his reaction when he had kissed her.

Jordan pulled into the station parking lot, and Jeremy bid his friend goodbye. "I hope to see you tomorrow."

Jordan tossed him a roguish smile, "Sure, I'll come. I'll see for myself the suffering you have to endure trying to escape from all those beautiful women."

* * *

Vikki conversed with her mother and sister on the porch enjoying lemonade and cookies. Her sister, Mary, refilled her glass and took a bite of her cookie. "So how do you like teaching?"

"It's fine now that I'm getting used to it. I was awfully nervous at first, but I've met some really nice people, especially Lisa, who teaches across the hall."

"And how do you like being a landlady?" her mother asked.

"Oh, fine. It's working out well."

As she spoke, her renter, with daughter in tow, rounded the corner from the back of the house. Vikki's heart skipped a beat when she saw him, and she gestured for him to come up. "Hi, how are you?"

"Sorry, I don't mean to interrupt, but—," he hesitated, "you left your sweater on the chair last night." He handed the sweater to her with a slight lift of his shoulders.

"Oh, thanks, um… this is my mother and my sister, Mary." She turned toward them, "Mom and Mary, this is Jeremy and his daughter, Heather. They rent the apartment upstairs."

Mary glanced at Heather curiously and then said to Jeremy, "I'm pleased to meet you."

"Hi," her mother added.

Jeremy offered his hand to both of them, "The pleasure is mine."

Mary smiled at him. "Would you like a cookie?"

"No, thanks, I won't bother you ladies any longer."

Mary glanced at her sister with merriment. "Oh, I'm sure it's no bother."

Vikki felt her cheeks grow warm and shot her sister a warning look. "Of course it isn't. You're welcome to stay and have some cookies."

"I want a cookie," Heather announced.

Jeremy flashed his endearing smile. "You may have one cookie, Heather, and remember to say thank you." He took a cookie from the plate and gave it to her.

"Thank you, Vikki."

"You are welcome, Honey."

"Vikki, come with us," the little girl requested.

Vikki smiled and twisted her necklace. "Maybe another time, ok?"

"Come on, Heather." Jeremy said. "Nice meeting you ladies. See you later, Vikki." He gave a little wave and bounded down the steps.

After Vikki sat down again, her sister gave her a meaningful look. "You didn't tell us your renter was such a cutie."

"Oh, do you think so? I've never really noticed," Vikki said, her wide eyes betraying her.

"Right." Mary giggled, "You seem to be on pretty friendly terms."

"It does look like you have become acquainted." Her mother glanced at the sweater in Vikki's hand. "Heather seemed to know you quite well."

"She does, and yes, he's a friend. I enjoy spending time with Heather," she said a tad too curtly.

"Oh, I see." Mary snickered. "You like spending time with Heather." The words brought forth another bout of giggles.

"Yes," Vikki replied, drawing the word out. "He's a friend. I don't understand what's so funny. At any rate, he doesn't want anything but friendship. He lost his wife three years ago, and he's still grieving over her death." She explained Shannon's murder, leaving out most of the details. Her mother and sister were quiet when Vikki finished.

"That's horrible," Mary spoke at last. "It's a wonder he has been able to care for his daughter and get through school."

"What if the time comes when he is ready for a more personal relationship. How would you feel about that?" Vikki's mother questioned.

"I don't know," Vikki confessed. "I think I would be competing with another woman, even if she is a memory." A troubled look shadowed her face. "I've been down that road before."

Mary touched her hand. "That's way different. In the first place, Tom was a jerk, and…"

"Maybe. But if I were just …"

"Don't say it," her mother interrupted. "There is nothing wrong with you. He would have cheated on anyone."

"Mother's right," Mary chimed in. "Tom would have found someone else no matter what you looked like or how perfect you were. He's a player and always will be." She squeezed Vikki's hand. "You are a very lovely girl." She gave her a gentle smile. "You're interested in Jeremy. I can see that. And who knows what will happen."

"A memory is difficult to let go, and besides, Jeremy feels guilty about not being able to save Shannon. I'm afraid he will never be able to love someone else like he did her." Vikki sat back down on the porch swing. "How are things with Robbie—that's his name, isn't it?" she asked to change the subject.

Robbie worked in the administration office of the hospital where Mary was employed. They had been dating for about three months. "Just fine," she smiled. "I really like him a lot."

"Did you tell me he played in a band?"

The three ladies conversed until Mary said she needed to run some errands before work. Vikki spent the rest of the afternoon cleaning her house, grading papers, and wondering why she couldn't get Jeremy off her mind.

CHAPTER TWELVE

J ordan arrived at New Life Community a few minutes before the service began, not leaving time to look up Jeremy. He took a seat on the end of a row a few feet down from a young woman sitting alone. During the time of greeting, the brunette extended her hand to him. He stood to greet her and took her hand. Her short dark wavy hair and amber eyes framed by long soft lashes made his heart skip a beat. "Hi," he replied and, realizing he was staring at her, quickly shifted his eyes to a point over her shoulder. "Nice to meet you." He smiled weakly and sat down. Well, unless Jeremy was blind, he surely couldn't have missed this girl. She was beautiful.

The music was uplifting, and Pastor Brandon's message was interesting enough that Jordan almost forgot about the dark-haired beauty a few feet from him. After the service ended, Jordan lost track of her in the crowd. *Oh well, she's probably taken anyway*, he thought.

"Hey, I'm glad you came." Jeremy walked up to Jordan and tapped his shoulder. "Did you enjoy the service?"

"It was good; I enjoyed it."

"Great, come on. I'll introduce you to some people." Jeremy motioned toward Pastor Brandon and his wife. "I'd like you to meet…"

Jordan spotted the girl from the service and elbowed Jeremy, "Hey, do you know that girl over there?"

"Where?" Jeremy answered, looking in the direction Jordan indicated.

"There, see that chick with the really great …. um, face?" he stammered.

Jeremy tilted his head, lifted his eyebrows, and half grinned at his friend. "The one with the really great face?"

"Well, you know—well put together," Jordan quipped in return.

Suddenly, realizing the girl Jordan was talking about, Jeremy gazed at him in wonder. "That chick with the really great," and he emphasized the next word, "*face*," is my sister.

Jordan mirrored Jeremy's look of surprise. "Oh, sorry, I didn't know—I didn't mean anything disrespectful. I sat near her during church and…" He paused for a second and then continued with mock seriousness in his tone. "Let's try this again. Hey Preacher, could you introduce me to that nice lady over there next to the bulletin rack. I sat beside her, and she seemed so enthralled by the message that I wanted to compare notes with her—you know, see if she got the same meaning from it that I did."

Jeremy chuckled at his friend's irreverence. "I'm not sure I want you to meet my sister."

Jessie lifted her head at the sound of his laughter, and Jeremy motioned her over. As she approached, he said, "Jessie, I'd like you to meet my friend and mentor at work, Jordan."

"Nice meeting you again." She smiled. "I believe we sat next to each other."

"Yes, we did, but now I know your name and you're my friend's sister," he winked playfully at Jeremy.

Jeremy shook his head, "I'll probably regret this, but Jessie and I are going out for a bite to eat. Would you like to join us?"

"Well, I'm not sure that that was the most gracious invitation I've ever received," he replied, flashing a smile at Jeremy's sister. "But I'd like to join you if that's ok with you, Jessie."

"Of course. We'd like that."

"Great. Where are you going?"

"How about Barney's?" Jeremy suggested.

"Sounds good, I'll meet you there." Jordan grinned.

Later that afternoon, Jordan sprawled in his overstuffed armchair, only half engaged in Sunday afternoon football. His mind drifted to the lunch date he had shared with Jeremy and Jessie. Jessie intrigued him. She was beautiful, intelligent, and not at all coy. Playing the field wasn't his style; he didn't want a different girl every few months. Most of the girls he'd gone out with were more interested in having a new boyfriend to parade around for a while.

Jessie, though, seemed different, yet he made that mistake before. Besides, she was a little too sophisticated for him. He had learned that Jessie had a job with a well-known retail chain, being one of the buyers of women's clothing. She had seemed genuinely interested in his job, but often women thought dating a paramedic or firefighter was exciting, though not what they had in mind as a career for a long-term boyfriend. Jessie was probably like most women he knew, wanting a guy with more money, more sophistication, and a more convenient work schedule. Besides that, Jessie was gorgeous. She could have any guy she wanted. He might as well face it. She was definitely out of his league. Feeling restless, he decided he needed to exercise. He put on his running shoes and headed out the door. A good run always helped him unwind.

* * *

Jessie had a promising future at just twenty-five years of age. Her job as a buyer was challenging, afforded some travel experiences, and paid very well. She had an apartment located on the north side of Indianapolis in an excellent neighborhood. She should be pleased with her life, and for the most part, she was. Still, something was missing. It wasn't a lack of social life. She had plenty of friends and wasn't lacking attention from men, but her life seemed empty. Her romances were often short-lived; she had not ever had a serious relationship. She was so busy trying to convince herself that she didn't need a man to take care of her, she didn't give anyone a chance to show he was interested in her more than as an adornment.

Her phone rang, and Jessie put down her book to answer it.

"Hello?"

"Hi, Jessie," said her brother. "What are you up to?"

"Oh, nothing much. Just reading a book."

"I just called to say it was good to see you at church. I wasn't expecting you."

"I enjoyed it last Sunday, so I decided to come again today."

"Well, I'm glad you did." He paused. "I hope you didn't mind Jordan joining us for lunch."

"No, not at all. Jordan seems like a nice guy. I enjoyed our conversation."

"Great. I think he might be interested in you."

To her surprise, she felt her heart quicken, and she sat up straighter. "Why? Did he tell you that?"

"No, I haven't talked to him since lunch, but I think it's pretty obvious."

"Really?"

"Yeah, really. I was wondering what I should say if he asked me about you. May I give him your number?"

"Well," Jessie hesitated, "What do you think of him? I mean what kind of guy is he?"

Jeremy laughed. "Mischievous, a bit irreverent, but sensitive underneath all the swagger. I really do like him. He's a great guy."

"He does seem like he would be fun to be around. I guess I'd see him again—if he asks. Do you think he's seeing anyone?"

"No, I don't think he dates around a lot. He strikes me as a one-woman man."

They talked a while longer, then said their goodbyes. Jessie hung up the phone, hoping she wouldn't regret saying she'd see Jordan. There was no denying that he was pleasant to look at, and he did have an engaging personality. She didn't suppose any harm could come from seeing him again. Anyway, she could use a little diversion, and she wasn't seeing anyone special. If he asked, she just might say yes.

CHAPTER THIRTEEN

Monday was not a great day. Vikki was only too glad for the bell to ring at 3:30. She crossed the hallway to Lisa's room. "My kids were worse than they've ever been," she proclaimed to Lisa. "My girls were in a snit, and Allison tattled from the moment she walked in the door."

Lisa looked up and nodded her head. "My kids were difficult today too. And it isn't even October yet." She gathered some papers to check from the tray behind her desk. "That kind of worries me."

"Well, all I know is, I can't handle that tattling all year." She glanced at Lisa and saw an ugly looking bruise about three inches long below her elbow. "Oh goodness, what happened to your arm?" She wondered why she hadn't noticed the black and blue splotch before.

"Oh, that." Lisa gave a nervous laugh, eyeing the bruise, "I whacked my arm against the stair rail when I was in a hurry cleaning the house yesterday. Can you believe that?"

"It looks awful. That must have been some whack. I bet that hurt."

"It sure did. My husband, Lee, couldn't believe it either." She collected her sweater from the chair and slipped her arms through the sleeves. "I'm just a klutz, I guess." She shuddered, "It's a little cool in here, isn't it?"

It wasn't until after she had gone to bed that night that Vikki recalled a conversation she had overheard a few days ago. She was in the workroom situated off the lounge but could hear the hushed conversation between two teachers.

"All I know is she's had too many accidents."

"Do you really think he hits her, though? Maybe she just bruises easily. I know some people do."

"I don't know, but it sure is suspicious, and I think she's been avoiding people."

The teachers left, and Vikki had almost forgotten the strange conversation, but now the words filled her with apprehension. Who had they been talking about? Could it have been Lisa?

Vikki was drifting off to sleep that night when an unsettling memory came to her mind. She had noticed that Lisa's eye was red and swollen about a week after school started but hadn't felt close enough to Lisa at that time to ask about it. She just assumed Lisa had hit her eye with something.

Well, the situation would bear watching, but Lisa didn't seem to fit the typical abuse victim. She was a confident and enthusiastic teacher, not timid or insecure. The bruise did seem a little peculiar, especially in light of the conversation she had overheard. Maybe her sister, Mary, would have some perspective to offer.

As it turned out, it was Jeremy that Vikki confided in about Lisa. Though Jeremy had kept his distance since the weekend, he appeared at her car Thursday afternoon as she was carting in her books.

"Here, let me help you," he offered, reaching out his hand.

Vikki handed him her canvas bag and reached in the car

for some more books. "Thanks, I never seem to get caught up."

"Would you like some help? I could probably grade some papers for you."

She laughed. "I'm sure you have better things to do with your time."

"Not, really," he assured her. "Anyway, Heather has been asking about you. We could come down after supper. Heather could play while I help you grade papers."

Vikki sensed he was serious about wanting to help, so she suggested Jeremy and Heather come for supper, and then he could help if he wanted. "Do you like spaghetti?"

"Sure," he said with an easy smile. "Let me bring a salad. I think I have a bag of lettuce in the fridge."

A little less than an hour later, Jeremy tapped on her stairway door. "Here we are," he said as Vikki opened the door.

Heather ran to Vikki with outstretched arms. "Here we are," she repeated her father's statement. Vikki felt Jeremy's eyes on her as she greeted Heather.

Jeremy dumped the salad in a bowl Vikki placed on the counter. He put plates on the table while she put the finishing touches on the meal. They talked casually about their week as they set the table.

After supper, Vikki cleared the table, so they had a place to work. She made plans for a project on sea animals, and Jeremy graded three stacks of papers. Heather played with an assortment of plastic bowls, spoons, and cups on the floor beside the table.

Close to an hour later, Vikki looked up at Jeremy. "Thanks for grading all those papers. It helped a lot."

"Glad to help. You must spend a lot of time working at home."

"The life of a teacher, I guess."

On an impulse, Vikki relayed to Jeremy the conversation she had heard in the lounge and told him about the bruise on Vikki's arm.

"That does sound suspicious, but you don't really have much to go on," Jeremy stated after hearing her out.

Vikki sat across from him at the table with her head propped on her fist. "I know, and she doesn't seem the type. She's a confident teacher and a leader in the school, but I guess that doesn't mean things are the same at home."

"Yeah, you're right, I've heard of cases where the woman is very good at covering up her abuse, and nobody knows for years," Jeremy offered. "They're often too afraid or ashamed to tell anyone."

Vikki sighed, "I guess it is something to keep an eye on."

"I'd say so." Jeremy raked his hand through his hair. "That's really all you can do until Lisa wants to talk."

Around 8 p.m., Jeremy said it was near Heather's bedtime. "Thanks for letting us eat dinner with you."

"Thanks again for grading all those papers, Jeremy. I would have been up late tonight finishing up."

"Anytime. I had a good evening." He paused and looked away for a second before bringing his focus back to her. "I think you've been feeling uncomfortable around me since last Saturday, and I'm sorry about that, because I really do want to be friends."

Vikki smiled, "I'd like that too, and I appreciate you telling me about Shannon. I know it was difficult for you."

Jeremy pushed back from the table and walked over to fetch his daughter. "Time to go, Angel. We've got to get you ready for bed." He paused and turned to Vikki. "I know you have your own church, but I'd love for you to come to New Life one Sunday."

"I might do that. I really wouldn't mind trying something

else. My church is about thirty minutes from here." Vikki smiled, a spark of interest in her eyes.

"How about this Sunday?"

"Well, ok. Let me know how to get there."

"You might as well ride with me. It will blow Alice's mind to see me walk in with a lovely lady. Alice is the senior pastor's wife. And" his blue eyes danced, "if she thinks you're my girlfriend, she might quit trying to fix me up with every available girl from the church."

Vikki put a finger to her chin. "Hmm, I guess I could ride in with you, if you don't think it will cause a problem."

His smile broadened. "I'm sure people will just marvel at my luck." He held her eyes for a lingering moment. "Goodbye."

"Bye, thanks again. I'll see you Sunday."

Vikki sighed as she walked back to the table to finish up her plans for the next day. She would have to be content being Jeremy's friend, even though her heart wished for more. She wondered if she would ever have a lasting relationship. Deception had ruined one already.

Unwanted memories, vivid and painful, rushed to her mind. Tom had entered her life during her sophomore year in college. Five years her senior, and working on his master's degree in Education, she had met him in the college library where she worked part-time. Charming, attractive, and egotistical, he claimed to love Vikki's unpretentious charm, and she had been flattered by his attention.

Their romance progressed quickly, and they married the following summer. Her parents had been concerned that she had two years of school to finish, but Tom had a teaching job, and their daughter seemed happier than they had ever seen her.

It was true; Vikki was happy, and she loved her husband. Comfortable with her perception that Tom's arrogance and self-absorption were forgivable personality traits, she was even a little awed that he had chosen her over others who were more outgoing and sophisticated.

Tom, however, became bored with his role as husband, wishing for the freedom of his former life. He had married on an impulse, seeking a new thrill. When the novelty wore off, he became restless.

It had been a month before their first anniversary when Vikki's perfect world collapsed, shattering her dreams and crushing her spirit. It was a Saturday evening and Tom had plans with his friends, as he often did, so Vikki invited her sister to go to dinner and catch a movie. After dinner at their favorite restaurant, they decided to forgo a movie and instead have girl time at Vikki's apartment. Nothing could have prepared her for the scene that assaulted her when she entered her home. Tom appeared in the hallway wearing only his jeans. "Vikki, what are you doing here?" he fumbled in shocked tones.

"We decided to spend time here instead of shopping. Why? What's wrong?" Vikki's stomach churned as the unthinkable slammed her thoughts. "What's going on?" she demanded.

"Vikki, I— - I didn't expect you home yet," Tom choked out.

A woman wearing one of Tom's shirts, and with bare legs, walked into the room, "Oh! I thought you said your wife was out of town." Her mouth opened in a condescending smile as if somehow Vikki was overreacting. "I guess I'd better get dressed. Sorry if I caused a problem."

Vikki gaped at her in stunned silence. Hot blood coursed through her veins, and a metallic taste formed on her tongue. Trembling with rage and with ferocity that shocked her, Vikki hurled herself against the girl, shoving her into the wall. "Get out now! Get out! Both of you!" She grabbed the woman, who was too startled to offer much resistance, and jerked her forward.

Tom grabbed Vikki's flailing arms from behind. "Stop Vikki! Don't push her again." His sharp voice pierced her heart.

Vikki spun around, "So, is this how you spend your weekends with friends?" she hurled. "Has our whole life been a lie? How many girls are there, huh?" She shook his arms. "Answer me!" Vikki slumped against the wall, hot tears streaming down her face.

Tom stared at her and shrugged. "I'm sorry you had to see this," but his voice held no sorrow.

Mary shoved in between them, "How dare you cheat on my sister!" She glared at him as if she might slap him across the face, "You need to get out now!" Tom and his girlfriend, who had quickly gotten her things together, left without a word.

Vikki felt her stomach lurch. She stumbled down the hallway to the bathroom and hung her head over the toilet. Mary slid down to the floor and held Vikki's hair away from her face while she heaved into the water. Vikki sat on the cold tile of the bathroom floor sobbing as her heart splintered into a thousand pieces. After her tears were spent, she dragged herself into her bedroom, numbly packed her suitcase, and walked out the door. Vikki demanded a quick divorce, and Tom readily agreed.

Vikki shook off the memories, completed her lesson plans, and showered.

As she got ready for bed, Lisa's bruised arm invaded her thoughts, and the realization that Lisa could be a victim of abuse troubled her. Vikki knew Jeremy was right about a person being afraid to admit they were in that situation. Tomorrow she would have to find some way to approach Lisa.

CHAPTER FOURTEEN

"Hey, Preacher, where've you been?" Jordan greeted Jeremy Thursday morning. "I was beginning to worry that you were staying away for good."

"I just wasn't scheduled much this week. Why would you think that?"

"Oh, I don't know," he quipped, "maybe to keep me away from your sister?"

"Now I wonder why you would imagine such a thing?" Jeremy teased.

"I'm not touching that line," Jordan smiled with his eyes and shook his head. "But seriously, I would like to see her again."

Jeremy shot him a knowing look. "I kind of figured, so I talked to Jessie, and I think she might go out with you."

Jordan's mouth opened in surprise, "You're kidding me. What did you tell her anyway?"

"That you were an incorrigible rogue and dangerous to her reputation." Jeremy tilted his head and grinned at his friend.

"Thanks a lot. You're quite amusing."

Jeremy shrugged. "I learn from the best." He tapped Jordan's shoulder. "Hey, I have an idea. Do you play cards?"

"A little poker now and then."

"Why don't we set up a card game? Jessie plays poker, and I believe my friend Vikki knows how to play, too."

Jordan gave him a quizzical look. "Who's Vikki?"

"Oh, she owns the apartment I rent."

Jordan squinted his eyes. "Your landlady? How old is she anyway?" he scoffed.

"Early twenties, I'd guess," Jeremy said casually and slipped his hands in his front pockets, "We've played Rummy a couple of times. I think she might know how to play poker."

Delightful surprise played on Jordan's features. "Whoa, Preacher Boy! You never told me you had a thing for your landlady. No wonder you aren't interested in the ladies at church." His eyes grew round, and his mouth gaped. "Hey, isn't your apartment above her house?"

"Yes, the apartment is on the second story," Jeremy stated matter-of-factly.

"Well, now, isn't that a convenient setup?" He gave Jeremy a light-hearted punch. "Is she pretty?"

Jeremy scowled. "Yes, it's a nice apartment, but I don't have a thing for her."

"Is she pretty?" Jordan persisted.

Jeremy shrugged. "I don't know. I've never really thought about it."

"Right," Jordan nodded. "Come on, you've played cards with her, and you didn't notice what she looked like?"

"Okay, she's pretty," Jeremy replied with an eye roll. "She has beautiful green eyes. Do you want me to ask Jessie, or not?"

"Sure, sounds fun. I wouldn't want to deny you an opportunity to stare into those beautiful green eyes." Jordan winked and sauntered toward his desk.

* * *

Jessie glanced at the clock above the radio as she turned into her apartment complex Friday evening. It was almost six. The get-together at her brother's apartment started at seven, meaning she had scarcely twenty minutes to get ready. She pulled on her favorite pair of jeans and a soft gray sweater. She tousled her short wavy hair and wondered why she had agreed to this date. True, Jordan was cute with his dark brown eyes and teasing smile, but he simply wasn't the type of guy she went for. Most of her dates were with ambitious men interested in making money and climbing the ladder of success. Maybe she was due for a change, though. Anyway, a card game with friends wasn't an evening of romance, and it might be the diversion she needed to get rid of her gloomy mood. She hurried out the door.

She turned into the drive of the old farmhouse directly behind Jordan. He lingered at the porch as she emerged from her car and greeted her with an easy smile. "Hi, Jessie. It is good to see you again."

Jessie smiled back at him. "I was looking forward to it. How are you doing tonight?"

"Just fine," he responded with another smile.

The two of them walked to the doorway where Vikki greeted them. "Come on in. I'm glad you both could make it. Jeremy will be here in a minute. He's dropping off Heather at her grandparents' house."

It was a fun evening. Jordan and Jeremy kept the laughter going with their bantering back and forth, and the four played until midnight before calling it quits.

While the girls were chatting after the last game, Jordan

motioned Jeremy over and gestured toward Vikki, "You're right, Preacher Boy, she does have beautiful green eyes."

Jeremy half-grinned, "I guess so."

"And don't be pretending you don't notice. I saw you looking at her with puppy dog eyes."

"Oh, I was not. You're crazy."

"Right," he razzed and thumped Jeremy on the shoulder.

As they were leaving, Jordan walked Jessie to her red Mustang. "Nice car you have there."

"Thanks, I saved a long time for it. I always wanted a Mustang."

Jordan hesitated at her door." It's awfully late," he voiced his concern. "Why don't you let me follow you until you get off these country roads?"

Jessie smiled. "I'll be okay, but thanks anyway."

"I don't mind, and I'd feel better if you let me follow you to the highway."

"I'm fine. No one needs to follow me. I'm often out this late, and I can take care of myself," Jessie said with a bit of edge to her voice. "I'll text Jeremy when I get home."

Jordan took her hand as she reached for the door handle, causing her to swing around and face him. "I'm sure you can," his voice was low yet definite, "But I am going to follow you to the main road. These country roads are pretty deserted at this time of night."

Jessie shrugged. "Suit yourself." Her eyes lifted and locked with his serious ones and her expression softened. "But I will be fine."

Jordan stood too close to her, yet his feet refused to move. Jessie's eyes shining in the light of the full moon worked their magic on him. Drawing her close, Jordan bent his head to kiss her cheek, but Jessie turned her face so that his lips delicately grazed hers. His lips met hers again in a soft, slow kiss. They stood there motionless in the warm early fall evening. Jordan held her shoulders in a light embrace.

It was Jordan who at last shattered the moment. "Hey," he said, taking a step back and flashing her a devilish smile, "I never kiss on the first date. You're going to ruin my reputation."

Jessie drew in a deep breath. "Well," she teased, "I guess it's really our second date if you count lunch last Sunday."

"So it is." Eyes twinkling, he brought her hands gently to his lips. She stirred him in a way he had never known before. "I think I'd better go now," he mumbled. He kept hold of her hands, not wanting the moment to end yet afraid for it to continue.

Jessie whispered, "Bye, Jordan."

"Maybe I'll see you at church Sunday," he said as he opened her car door.

Jessie only nodded. She got in her car and started the engine. Jordan tapped on her window, and she powered it down. "Wait for me, I'm still following you to the main road."

Jessie's lips curved up a little, "Suit yourself."

CHAPTER FIFTEEN

Vikki pulled into her school's parking lot Saturday morning. It was not uncommon for teachers to come to the school over the weekend to work in their rooms, so she wasn't surprised to see Lisa's car and another car she didn't recognize. Good, she thought, someone else is working today; she always felt a little uneasy when she was the only one in the building.

The fall day was breezy with a chill in the air. Vikki sprinted to the door and held up her keycard. She stopped by the lounge, dropped coins into the soda machine, and listened as the pop can rolled down the chute. On impulse, she bought Lisa's favorite cola. Vikki collected her cans and strolled to her classroom at the end of the hall. She would offer a drink to Lisa and then begin the long process of making plans for the next week.

As Vikki walked toward her room, she heard an angry male voice coming from the end of the hallway. Her pace slowed as she drew closer. The shouting came from Lisa's room.

"Don't you ever walk away from me again! Do you understand me?" the voice growled.

"Okay, okay, let go, you're hurting me," a woman whimpered.

Vikki heard the sound of a hand smacking against flesh and a low sob. "I'm sick of this school taking all your time," the male voice bellowed. There was a thud and a rattle as if someone had fallen against the closet doors that lined the classroom's back wall.

Vikki stood frozen to the floor. Her first impulse was to turn and run down the hall, but that was unthinkable. Needing to create a diversion, something that would warn of her approach, she hurled the pop cans to the floor. They skidded down the hall, slid past the last two rooms, and crashed into the wall. The clatter produced the desired results. Lisa's room grew eerily quiet.

Vikki hurried down the hall to collect the cans. Lisa and a man with graying hair peered out the classroom door. "Oh, how clumsy of me," Vikki stammered. Avoiding their stares, she mumbled, "I must have tripped over my own feet. I'm sorry if I scared you. I just came to get a little work done."

Alarm flashed in the man's eyes, but his smile was arrogant. "No, you didn't scare us. We were just afraid you had hurt yourself. I'm Lee Bannister, Lisa's husband," he said, offering his hand.

"I'm Vikki. I teach across the hall," she croaked out and shook his hand.

"Well, I guess she's not the only clumsy one," Lee gestured toward Lisa. "My wife just fell against the closet door and banged her eye. I'm afraid it might be bruised."

Vikki turned to Lisa, a queasy feeling mounting in her gut. "Oh! It does look like you're getting a black eye. I'll go down to the lounge for some ice."

Lisa spoke for the first time. "That won't be necessary,

Vikki. I don't really think it's that bad." She sniffled and attempted a smile. "I see you have some work to do also."

"Well, I guess I'd better leave you two to get that work done, so you'll have some of your Saturday left," Lee stated as if nothing was out of the ordinary. He glanced at Lisa's eye.

"You might want to get some ice on that after all. I need to get going." He kissed his wife on the cheek and stalked down the hall.

Vikki waited for a minute staring at Lee until he reached the door and left the building. She turned to look at Lisa, "Are you okay?" It was an absurd question, but all she could think to say.

"I'm fine. I just fell, like my husband said."

Vikki dropped her gaze and touched her cross necklace, searching for the right words. She looked up and met Lisa's eyes, "I heard it, Lisa. I was coming down the hall when I heard him shouting. I didn't know what to do, so I threw my pop cans to make noise." She paused. "I know he hit you."

Lisa's face contorted, and she wrung her hands. "Vikki, you don't understand. He's not like that. It's just—he's under a lot of pressure right now."

"It's not the first time, is it, Lisa? I've seen bruises before," Vikki paused, "and I've overheard talk in the lounge."

Vikki saw the shock pass over Lisa's face.

"Please, don't tell anyone," she begged. "I can handle this. My... My husband is a leader in the community and at our church, and we belong to several social groups. This is a small town, Vikki. Talk is cheap."

Vikki shook her head. She couldn't believe Lisa's words. "I'm going to get ice. Your eye looks terrible." She hurried down the hall and snatched a sandwich bag from the lounge cabinet. She grabbed some ice in the freezer tray and dropped four cubes in the bag. Short of breath from rushing back to the room, Vikki gave the bag to her friend. "I don't understand, Lisa. Why would you put up with that kind of treatment? You deserve better."

"I told you. I have a lot at stake. I live in a beautiful house. I can have any material thing I desire, and Lee is respected in the community. Besides, he usually treats me very well." She glanced at the sparkling diamond on her finger as if it offered proof of his devotion. "You know all men have a limit when they get angry. Lee just has a hot temper." She gingerly touched her eye. "I'll admit it's been worse lately." Her lip trembled, "He never used to get this physical, but I think he is under a lot of stress at work."

"That's ridiculous," Vikki asserted, "I was married to a real jerk. He was immature, arrogant, and even unfaithful. But he never hit me. If a man ever laid a hand on me, it would be the last time. I can't believe you would tolerate that kind of treatment." Vikki's face flushed as she spoke the bold words.

Lisa hesitated. "Maybe you're right, but I'd have nothing without him."

Vikki gaped at her. "You have a good job. You can take care of yourself. What makes you want to stay?"

Lisa bristled. "I am married, you know. We have a child. I don't know if I'm ready to throw it all away."

Vikki sighed. "Well, at least move out for a while. Let him know you won't put up with his behavior. You can move in with me for a few weeks if you want."

Lisa shook her head. "He just needs to find an outlet for his temper. I've been after him to take up golf again."

Or boxing, Vikki sneered to herself. Not knowing what else to say and worried that she might have pushed too hard, Vikki decided to let the matter drop for now. "I'm going to try to get some work done." Her voice softened. "If you want to talk, you know where to find me."

Vikki had difficulty concentrating on her work. She wondered how Lisa could function at all. Why a person would choose to live with a man like that was beyond her. She sighed and tucked her hair behind her ear. Her plans were never going to get finished unless she got busy.

She had worked for about an hour when Lisa appeared at her door. "I'm leaving now. I guess I'll see you later."

"Bye," Vikki met her gaze, "Again, if you need to talk or a place to stay, call me anytime."

"Okay." Lisa turned to leave and then looked back at Vikki. "I know you're trying to help me, and I appreciate that, but I'll be all right." Her smile was feeble as she turned and walked away.

Vikki finished her work and headed home. Halfway there, she released her death grip on the steering wheel and stretched her fingers. Lisa needed help but was afraid to let anyone know about Lee's abusive behavior. At any rate, Vikki didn't know who to tell. She didn't know Lisa's family, friends, or even where Lisa lived. Turning in her drive, she decided she would talk to Jeremy. Maybe he knew of a good Christian counselor or would have another idea of how to help.

After eating a light lunch and cleaning up the kitchen, Vikki called Jeremy to see if he had time to talk.

"Sure, Heather is napping, so why don't you come on up?"

"Will I be interfering with your studying?"

"Not at all. I'm not preaching tomorrow, so all I have to prepare for is my Sunday School lesson. Besides, I'd rather spend time with you."

"Okay, if you're sure. I'll be there in a few minutes."

Jeremy greeted Vikki at the door. "Hi, come in." He led her to the kitchen table. "Would you like a glass of tea or a soda?"

"Tea would be fine."

They chatted for a few minutes, and then Jeremy placed

his hands on the table. "When you called you seemed to have something you wanted to talk about."

"Something happened when I was at school this morning. I just need to talk through it with someone."

"Sure, what's up?"

Jeremy listened as Vikki told of the morning's events. "I just don't know what to do," she finished with a shake of her head and stared at her clasped hands.

Jeremy considered her words. "You've offered her a way out. I'm not sure what else you can do since she doesn't want to report him."

"But what if he really hurts her next time? I'd never forgive myself for doing nothing." Dismay washed over her face.

Jeremy reached for her hands across the table. "You wouldn't be to blame, Vikki. Lisa has to make the decision to get help. All you can do is be there for her and support her if she decides to report her husband's abuse."

Vikki nodded. "I guess you're right. I just hope he doesn't hurt her again."

"Me too. I think New Life has a list of Christian counselors in the community. I'll see what I can find out."

Vikki thanked him and they talked for a few more minutes. Then she said goodbye so Jeremy could finish his lesson before Heather woke up.

"Are you still planning on coming to church with me tomorrow?"

"Sure," Vikki smiled. "And thanks for talking to me."

"No problem, I just wish I could have been more helpful."

"You were—just by listening. Text me in the morning when you're ready to leave."

Getting ready for church Sunday morning, Vikki gave the pile of clothes a dark look and tugged on the sleeve of the pink sweater she had tossed on the bed. She pulled it over her head, turned to the side, and examined her reflection in the mirror. Dressed only in her sweater and underwear, Vikki scowled at her image and gave herself a little jab. Even though she wasn't overweight, her stomach was not completely flat. It rounded into a bit of a bulge. Her clothing would help hide the slight bump, but it was there just the same. She pulled on her pants, ran her fingers through her unruly hair, and studied her face. She was attractive enough, she supposed, but it was her secret fantasy to be the kind of girl that turned men's heads. She knew that it was silly, some would even say sinful, but she only wished to be found desirable. The fact that she wanted one man, a preacher no less, to see her in that way gave her a stab of guilt. Not that it mattered anyway, Jeremy wasn't looking for romance. He had made that clear.

* * *

Vikki walked down her porch steps to meet Jeremy after his text. "Hi, how are you?"

"I'm fine." Jeremy eyed her sweater sleeve and pulled out a small white bundle. "That's a nice sweater, but do you really need this," he said with a grin.

Vikki felt her face color, and she snatched the wad from his hand. "Oh! It's just a sock."

Jeremy laughed, his eyes playful, "And just what did you think it was?"

She lifted her chin. "Never mind."

Jeremy's face wore a tease. She returned it with a smile, and her green eyes shone as they met his.

Jeremy held her gaze for a long moment. He wondered if she was aware of what she did to him, how those green eyes messed with his heart. Thoughts of the evening on his balcony came to his mind. He remembered the softness of her skin on his fingers as he stroked her cheek, her wide eyes looking into his, and the taste of her sweet lips.

Heather grew impatient waiting in her car seat and interrupted his thoughts. "Come on, Daddy," she demanded. Jeremy broke his gaze and waved at his daughter. "Okay, we're coming. Let's get going."

Jeremy and Vikki walked up the sidewalk to the church with Heather between them, each holding one of her hands. Arriving a few minutes early, they dropped Heather off in the preschool classroom and headed down the hall to one of the adult classrooms. Two rows of long narrow tables with chairs on the backside faced a whiteboard. Vikki sat down at the far end of the table and waited as Jeremy found a can of pencils and placed them and his stack of handouts at the end of the table closest to the front of the room. He took a chair and turned it around so that he was facing Vikki. They quietly conversed while they waited for the class members to arrive.

Alice walked through the door first. She smiled a greeting to Vikki and gave Jeremy a curious glance.

Jeremy caught her look. "Alice, this is my friend Vikki. Vikki, this is Alice. She's our senior pastor's wife."

Alice introduced Vikki to a few close-by class members and took a seat. Vikki, a little embarrassed by all the attention, greeted each person and then sat quietly pretending to be interested in the papers in front of her.

Alice flashed Jeremy a sly look. Jeremy narrowed his eyes, catching her silent remark. That woman never gave up. Well, let her think what she wanted. If she had the idea that Vikki was more than a friend, so be it. At least he could quit worrying about her fixing him up with someone from church.

* * *

The class Jeremy led was a study in Christian living. The lesson engaged the group, and the discussion was lively. Vikki felt herself relaxing enough to enjoy the comments of those gathered around the tables.

She was looking for a particular verse Jeremy had suggested when she felt the peculiar sensation of someone watching her. Glancing down the table, she saw a man quickly shift his eyes away from her. Though only catching a glimpse of his face, he was somehow familiar. She flipped through her Bible aimlessly, fighting the impulse to look down the table again. Unable to restrain her curiosity, she stole a peek. Yes, she knew that man, but where had she seen him? A feeling of unease nagged at her for the rest of the class.

As she gathered her purse and Bible to leave, she again felt someone's eyes on her. This time when she turned her head, she found the man looking directly, and not kindly, at her. Aware that she had noticed his scrutiny, he gave a slight nod and turned to leave the room. Recognition sent a shiver down her spine. It was Lisa's husband. She studied the doorway, unable to believe it was him. Maybe he just looked like Lisa's husband.

Jeremy touched Vikki's arm. "What is it?" he asked. "You look upset. Are you okay?"

"Jeremy, who is that guy that was sitting at the end of the table?" she whispered. "He was tall with grayish hair."

"Lee Banister, an elder. Why?"

It *was* him. "That's Lisa's husband," she said under her breath.

"Yes, his wife is named Lisa. Why? Do you know him?"

"Lisa Bannister is the teacher I was telling you about, the one whose husband beats her."

Jeremy caught his breath, and his face wore an expression of shock. "Vikki, are you sure?"

Vikki clutched his arm; her voice was insistent. "It's him. I told you her name is Lisa Bannister."

"All right. Do you think he recognized you?"

"I'm sure of it. He was watching me during class."

As they walked out the classroom door, Jeremy said in a hushed voice, "I don't know Lee very well. He isn't all that friendly with me, but he doesn't seem like the kind of guy who beats his wife. Let me talk to Brandon later. Maybe he can shed some light on this situation. Right now, I need to get to the sanctuary. I'll show you where I sit, then after I read the scripture, I'll join you."

As they moved toward the room, Vikki spotted Lee ahead of them. She didn't see Lisa anywhere, but no wonder; people would notice her black eye. She saw Lee take a seat near the front on the same side Jeremy had indicated. Jeremy led her to the first row and sat on the end, positioning themselves two rows directly in front of Lee. A shiver ran up her spine at the thought of him staring at her from behind.

Jeremy followed Vikki's eyes and whispered, "I'm sorry, Vikki. I need to sit here, but if you want you can move back, and I'll try to join you later."

She wavered for a few seconds. "No, it's okay. I'll be fine." She would concentrate on the service and try to forget who sat behind her.

"Hey, do you mind if we scoot in here?" a familiar voice asked. "You look kind of lonely."

As she turned her head, relief and surprise rushed over her. "Please do," she smiled and gestured to Jordan and Jessie. "I didn't know you two were coming. I would enjoy your company." That statement was truer than they knew.

Vikki let them cross in front, and it occurred to her that they made a cute couple. She wondered if Jeremy thought the same. She knew from the way they interacted at the card game Friday that Jeremy and his sister were very close. He must think a lot of Jordan, or he wouldn't have encouraged their relationship by inviting both of them to play cards. And now they had come to church together.

Jessie certainly shared Jeremy's good looks. Though her hair was a darker color, they had a strong resemblance otherwise. She was surprised she hadn't noticed that the day Jessie was helping Jeremy move into the apartment instead of assuming she was his girlfriend.

Jeremy had finished the scripture reading and settled into the seat beside Vikki. He leaned over to greet Jessie and Jordan. "Hi, I'm glad you guys came today. Maybe we can get lunch after church."

"Jessie drove her car and we met here, but sure it sounds good." Jordan gave Jessie a sideways glance. "Would that be okay with you?"

Jessie nodded as they bowed for prayer.

Within the security of her friends, Vikki was able to concentrate on the service. It wasn't until they were leaving the sanctuary that she saw Lee again. After the four of them entered the lobby, Vikki excused herself and walked down the hallway leading to the restrooms. As she exited the lady's room, she almost bumped into Lee. He must have followed her. "Oh," she gasped as her hand flew to her chest.

He studied her with a stony look and asked bluntly. "You're Vikki, the teacher I met yesterday, aren't you?" When Vikki forced a nod, he continued. "Lisa's fall ended up giving her a black eye, so she decided to stay home this morning. I thought you might like to know."

Vikki considered fleeing but, instead, stood quietly, feigning indifference. He paused, seemingly unnerved by her aloofness, moved in closer, and his voice took on a patron-izing tone. "You probably wondered what was going on yesterday. I imagine it was a little alarming for someone like you. But you really don't need to worry your little head about it anymore. Things aren't always as they appear."

Vikki forced herself to look at his face. "Is that right?" She sensed he was searching for a sign of intimidation, but her face was cold.

Anger flickered across his face; his hand rose slightly, then quickly jerked back. Her eyes, deep green and oversized, betrayed her attempt to appear nonchalant. His mouth curved in an arrogant smile, and his eyes were dark, cruel orbs. "I wouldn't play with fire if I were you," he smirked. "'Have a nice day, Vikki." He turned and strutted away.

Vikki watched him until he turned the corner, then on wobbly legs headed back to the lobby. Jeremy met her halfway, "What's wrong? You're white as a sheet. Are you sick?" Concern shadowed his eyes.

"I'll be all right. May we leave, now? I really need to get out of here."

"Sure, I need to find Jessie first, though. She has Heather with her."

CHAPTER SIXTEEN

"Thanks for riding to the restaurant with me," Jordan said as he pulled alongside Jessie's Mustang in the church parking lot.

"I had a good time." Jessie replied. "I enjoyed the sermon today, too."

"So did I," he smiled and squeezed her hand.

New Life Community Church was situated on a five-acre lot bordering the town park. A walking trail meandered through the park, following a winding creek. "I know you have to work this afternoon, but do you think you have time for a walk?" Jessie asked.

Jordan jumped at the idea. "I think I can work it into my schedule."

The trail followed the church property's edge for a few feet and then winded down to the creek bed. The path curved downward to the blue water shimmering in the sun and followed its bank for a few hundred feet before turning away again. Jordan knew the place well.

The couple strolled down to the creek and walked along the bank for a few feet. Memories of days gone by played in

Jordan's mind. "My father and I used to come here when I was a child."

"Were they good times?"

"Yes, my father used to bring me to this park. We would hike down to the creek, and he taught me how to skip rocks. My dad wasn't overly affectionate, but when we were together here, he was different somehow. He talked to me about having honor and integrity. That was his way of showing me love, I guess." Jordan stopped, picked up a smooth stone, and skipped it across the water. "Sometimes I wish I could relive those times, go back to when I was twelve or so, before..." his voice trailed off.

Jessie grabbed a stone, flung it over the water and watched it sink. "Before what?"

Jordan ruffed the dirt with a stick. "My father died in an accident when I was thirteen."

"Oh, I'm sorry. We don't have to stay here if it bothers you."

"No, it's okay. I used to come here often to sort things out, but I haven't for a while." He picked up another stone. "It's all in the wrists—four times," he said as he lobbed it across the water and counted four splashes. "It seems so long ago now. It's been almost twelve years."

"Did your mother ever remarry?"

"Yes, when I was seventeen."

"And?"

Jordan's lips turned down a little, and he shrugged. "He's a good guy and he treats my mom and me well, but he's not my dad. Don't get me wrong. I love him, and he helped steady me when I was a teenager. I feel kinda bad that I don't have the same connection with him. I guess I just still miss my father."

"Well, you lost your dad at a very crucial time in your life." She paused and looked at him.

"Yeah, you're right. It was a super hard time. My dad made me who I am. He was honorable and kind. I only hope I can be half the man he was."

"So, you are unable to completely accept anyone else in your father's role because he filled it so well. I don't think that is so unusual."

Jordan sat silently, mulling over Jessie's words a moment, then patted her knee. "Not only are you beautiful, you're very perceptive." A rare blush swept Jessie's cheeks. Jordan gave her a playful grin. "And I bet with you around, I'll be able to stop visiting my shrink."

"Very funny." She brushed his hand off her knee and smothered a grin.

Jordan turned toward her. "Tell me about your childhood. Is your family close?"

"Yes, we are very close. My dad is a preacher and though we often disagreed about church doctrine as I grew older, he always let me have my say. He accepted and even encouraged our discussions as long as we were respectful."

"He sounds like a cool father."

"Yes, he's a great guy."

They talked about childhood memories and their families. Twenty minutes later, Jordan reluctantly decided they'd better head back if he wanted to get to work on time. As they began the walk to the car, Jessie slipped her hand into Jordan's. He closed his fingers around it, swinging her arm as they walked.

Jordan turned to face Jessie when they arrived at the parking lot. Taking her other hand, he pulled her close. Her face smiled up at him. Could a woman like Jessie be attracted to him? She was sophisticated and beautiful, definitely out of his league. Yet here she was in his embrace. As his eyes caressed her face, he felt drawn to her in a way he had never known. He had been in relationships before, had even thought he was in love a couple of times, but no one had ever captivated him like the girl he now held in his arms. "Jessie," he murmured, "I know we haven't known each other very long, but I feel like I've known you forever. I would like to keep seeing you." He waited a few seconds. "I know it might be crazy."

She tilted her head and gave him a curious look. "Why is it crazy? Anyway, you'll have to see me again. I want you to teach me how to skip rocks."

"I mean," he stumbled on his words. "You're beautiful. You work at an impressive job and make lots of money. Jeremy told me you were a buyer for some big retail chain."

"So?" She wrinkled her forehead.

"I'm just a regular guy, not the type you need. I don't have a prestigious job or make the kind of money you do. I'm sure you are used to a different sort of guy, like an executive type with a good job and lots of potential."

Jessie stepped back and shot him a look laced with frustration. "Listen, I work in an industry that supplies material things, things people want, but don't need. You save lives, Jordan. What do you think is more important? And," she went on, her eyes fiery. "I'm not looking for someone to fulfill a need. All I've ever wanted is an equal partner. If you have a problem with me making more money than you, then we need to stop this relationship before it goes any further." She spun away and marched to her car.

"Wait a minute!" Jordan sprinted ahead to her car and propped himself against the door, blocking her entrance. He raised his eyebrows and shot her a flirtatious smile. "My, aren't we spunky." She opened her mouth to speak, but he gently put his finger on her lips. "I didn't mean to imply that you needed anyone. But just maybe I need you."

He reached for her hands, and his expression grew serious. "I don't care if you make ten times more money than me.

I'm surprised that you'd be interested in a guy like me, that's all."

Jessie's face softened. "Why not? I'm weary of all the arrogant and pretentious men who care only about climbing the proverbial ladder of success—ones who don't worry about who they trample. The men I usually date care more about being adorned with a pretty decoration, or dating a woman with an influential family, than being in a meaningful relationship. You're different. You're funny, kind, and you care about others." A smile lit up her face. "And, besides, you're easy on the eyes. Why wouldn't I be attracted to you?"

"Well, when you put it that way," he held her shoulders, "I can't argue." He framed her face with his hands, and his lips met hers in a lingering kiss. After pulling away, he added, "I've never felt this way about anyone before." He twisted one of her waves around his finger. "I think I'm falling in love with you."

Jessie's eyes glowed with a mixture of surprise and apprehension. "You don't really know me, Jordan. I may not be the girl you think I am."

"Maybe not," he leaned against the car, "but then I don't have many preconceived notions about who you should be. I know you're a Christian, and that's the most important thing. You're also beautiful, kind, fun, and... spunky." He tipped his head and smiled at her. "I can't imagine learning anything that could make me feel differently about you."

Jessie bit her bottom lip and stared down at her shoes. Then, she backed up a little.

Jordan lifted her chin and gave her a tender look. "Hey, we've got plenty of time to get acquainted. I didn't mean to scare you off."

Her smile was faint. "Okay, but we'd better go now or you'll be late for work."

* * *

Jeremy stretched out on the floor with Heather as she climbed on and over him. He scooped her up over his head and swept her through the air like an airplane triggering shrieks of joy.

There was a knock on the kitchen door. "Vikki!" squealed the little girl.

"It must be Vikki," Jeremy agreed. He wondered if she was ready to talk. She was quiet during lunch. When he'd ask her on the drive home if she was upset, she had put him off, saying she would tell him about it later. Not wanting to pressure her, he had let the matter drop for the time being. However, he was sure she was upset about spotting Lee at church.

He opened the door. "Hi, Vikki, come on in."

"Vikki," Heather cried and ran to her for a hug.

"Hi, Heather, how are you doing?"

"I'm playing with my dolls," was her happy response, and she hurried over to them.

"Do you have a few minutes? I'm sorry I didn't call first. I need to talk to you about something."

"Sure, I was playing around with Heather, but it looks like she's moved on to more interesting toys." He led her to the table and got two bottles of water out of the refrigerator.

"You're upset about seeing Lee at church, aren't you?" He handed her a bottle and sat down across from her.

"It's not just that. When I went to the restroom after church, I think he followed me. When I came out, he was there waiting by the door."

Jeremy fixed his eyes on her. "What did he want?"

"I think he was there to intimidate me."

Jeremy took a sip of water. "Why do you think that?" he prompted.

Vikki described her encounter with Lee, emphasizing how he smirked at her and his tone of voice. As Jeremy listened, an uneasiness crept over him. He should speak to Brandon, the senior minister, about this. Vikki was a little self-conscious at times, but he knew she was not prone to paranoia. "I'll talk to Brandon tomorrow morning. He usually takes Mondays off, but maybe he'll meet me for coffee in the afternoon. This doesn't sound right. I mean, I admit I thought you might have misunderstood the situation at school, but now after hearing how he cornered you, I think there is a problem."

"I'm sorry to be such a bother," Vikki said, twisting the cap on her water bottle.

Jeremy shook his head, seeing the worry in her eyes. How could she ever imagine that she was a bother? "That's silly." He gazed at her. "You're never a bother. You're worried about your friend and rightfully so. I want to help if I can."

"Thanks. I'd better go now and get some work done. See you later."

Jeremy walked with her to the door and closed his fingers around her hand. "I'll call you tomorrow after I talk to Brandon."

"Okay, I should be home around 4:30." Her smile didn't reach her eyes. "Thanks for being a friend." She freed her hand from his grasp and took the steps to her living room.

* * *

"Your friend must have misunderstood the situation," Brandon declared after listening to Jeremy's account of Lee hitting his wife and his threatening behavior toward Vikki. "I've known Lee for years, and I can't imagine him abusing his wife." He frowned and took a sip of his coffee. "He's a good Christian man, one of our elders. You know that." He pursed his lips and set his cup down with a clunk.

Jeremy blew out a puff of breath, "I appreciate your reluctance to believe an elder in our church could be an abuser, but Lisa did admit to Vikki that Lee hit her. And she said he had become more physical lately." He looked at Brandon straight on. "Maybe Lee is a master of deception."

Brandon returned the look. "Jeremy, how long have you known Vikki?"

"Just a couple of months." Jeremy paused and wrapped his hands around his coffee mug. He guessed where this line of questioning was going. "But I can assure you, she's an honest, trustworthy person, and I don't believe she's inclined to overreact."

"And," Brandon gave Jeremy a deliberate stare, "my wife tells me she's quite lovely. Perhaps you're kind of taken with her?" He took a bite of the cherry pie he had ordered.

Jeremy raked his hand across his forehead and bit the insides of his cheeks in frustration. "I fail to see the significance of that remark. It clearly has nothing to do with this."

"I think you probably do see it."

"Then, obviously, I'm wasting my time," Jeremy snapped back. He slid his dessert away, no longer hungry.

Brandon wore the look of someone who knew he had overstepped his boundary. "Listen, Jeremy," he clasped his hands on the table, "I'm sorry. I shouldn't have made that last comment, but I've known Lee for years. He has never given me a reason to believe that his behavior toward his wife is anything but honorable. On the contrary, he's very protective of her. And," he lowered his voice, "she has had some problems."

"What kind of problems?"

"Well, she's kind of high strung. She often suffers from headaches, and Lee says she battles depression."

Jeremy studied Brandon, his blue eyes darkening. "I understand how you would have a difficult time with this. I don't even know Lisa. She certainly may have a lot of problems." He leaned forward with his elbows on the table, "But Vikki heard them argue. She saw the black eye, Brandon. I don't think Vikki could misinterpret that."

Brandon took another sip of coffee, put the cup down, and sighed. "Okay, Jeremy, I'll consider what you've told me, and I will try to watch the situation. I'll ask Lee how Lisa's doing, but I'm not ready to accuse or even suggest I have suspicions about him abusing her. I'm not saying your friend is making things up. I just believe she might have misunderstood the situation."

Jeremy crossed his arms and leaned back in his chair. "Thank you, for listening to me," he said with a trace of sarcasm. "I just felt I needed to advise you of the situation."

"And I thank you for that. I do respect your opinions," Brandon replied. He propped his chin on the fingers of his left hand. "By the way, just what is your relationship with Vikki?"

"She's my landlady and a friend," Jeremy answered coldly.

Brandon gave a slight nod. "I see."

Jeremy shoved away from the table, grabbed his check, and left Brandon staring after him.

* * *

As it turned out, Lee came to Brandon. He called his home that evening. "Do you have a few minutes? I need to talk to you about a situation that's come up, and I really need to meet with you in person."

"Sure," Brandon replied. "I can meet you at the church if you'd like. I was planning on working in my office tonight. Could you be there in about thirty minutes?"

"That would be ideal. I'll be there."

Brandon met Lee at the door, and they made their way to Brandon's office. He motioned for Lee to take the seat in front of his desk and sat down opposite him.

After exchanging pleasantries, Brandon asked, "What's up, Lee?"

"Well, I believe our associate pastor's girlfriend may have formed a low opinion of me."

"I'm not aware Jeremy has a girlfriend." Brandon replied.

"Oh, you know," Lee's voice was impatient, "the girl he brought to church with him on Sunday. Anyway, I can tell you she has misunderstood a situation concerning my wife."

"Oh, in what way?" Lee's statement piqued Brandon's interest.

"She teaches at school with Lisa, and apparently she thinks I'm a wife-beater."

Brandon raised his eyebrows. "Why would she think that?"

Lee shifted in his seat. "She overheard Lisa and me arguing at Lisa's school Saturday afternoon, and I'm afraid she thinks I hit Lisa." He paused as if he wasn't sure whether to continue. His voice lowered. "Actually, Lisa lunged at *me*, tripped over a box, and hit her cheek on the handle of her closet door." The corners of his mouth sagged, and he sighed. "I'm really worried about her. She's in a deep depression like before, and I'm worried that she might hurt herself again."

"Hurt herself again? What do you mean?" Brandon asked, intrigued.

Lee sported an expression of hopelessness, leaned in toward Brandon, and spoke in hushed tones. "You know I've spoken of Lisa's bouts with depression in the past, but nobody knows that Lisa has a history of psychotic behavior. Several years ago, she had a very serious spell and was hospitalized for a few days. She actually hurt herself on purpose, in some weird way to get attention." He sighed and shook his head. "I thought that was behind us, but now I've started noticing signs of it again."

Brandon kept his face void of expression and looked down at his desk, attempting to gain perspective in light of the conversation he'd had with Jeremy. Lee's story certainly explained how Vikki could have gotten the wrong impression of the situation. He raised his head. "Are you saying that Lisa lied to Vikki telling her that you hit her, and that she actually harmed herself?"

"Not necessarily lied. More of a manipulation, I'd say. She's a pro at setting things up to appear to be different than they really are. I'm sure she's convinced Vikki that I'm beating her. She may believe it herself. She is not in touch with reality."

"But, doesn't that affect her ability to teach?"

"Eventually, it will, if she doesn't get help. I've already set up an appointment with her doctor. He'll probably adjust her medicine again."

The two men talked a few minutes longer. Then, Lee stood up to leave. "I really appreciate you coming out to meet me like this. I needed to set this straight before you heard it from someone else."

Brandon didn't mention his conversation with Jeremy. "No problem. I'm glad you told me. If there is anything I can do, let me know. I know some excellent Christian counselors."

Brandon leaned back on his chair after Lee left, contemplating this new information. Everything was clear now. Lisa had persuaded Vikki that Lee hit her. No wonder Vikki had felt threatened by Lee when he confronted her at church as Jeremy had related to him. She must have misread his intentions since Lisa had portrayed him as a wife-beater.

Still, Brandon could not dismiss Jeremy's accusations.

What if Lee was lying? What if he had beat his wife and made up an elaborate tale of her suffering from a mental illness? No, Lee would never do that. Everyone in the church knew how he had stood by his wife over the years, sheltering her from rumors that she was not capable of being an adequate wife and mother. But could Lee be the source of these rumors? He tried to dismiss the accusations Vikki had made, but they remained tucked in the corner of his mind.

* * *

Lee gripped the steering wheel as several thoughts clamored for his attention. He was a man with a couple of serious problems. Hopefully, he had squelched the first one. Brandon trusted him; Lee was certain of that. He was also sure that Vikki had told Jeremy all about the little incident at school, but clearly, he hadn't talked to Brandon about it. At least, Brandon had not given any indication that he suspected anything.

Now he must deal with his other predicament. He had been stunned without a doubt last Sunday. It was to his fortune that Jessie hadn't seen him at church. Why had he not made the connection before? The last name, Marcus, was not very common. He should have put two and two together. Still, he wondered why he hadn't seen her before. He was sure she didn't attend regularly. He wouldn't have guessed that she was the religious type, but maybe she had mentioned something about going to church. Yes, now he remembered. She was a preacher's daughter. She had mentioned her brother was studying for the ministry. He'd seen them talking yesterday, and the resemblance was unmistakable.

Everything had gone awry since that young upstart of a pastor had taken a position at the church. First, his meddlesome girlfriend went poking around in things that were none of her business, and second, his sister turned out to be Jessie Marcus, of all people. He struck the dashboard as he remembered the last encounter he'd had with Jessie. Somehow, he needed to get rid of that preacher and his sister and Vikki. Together they could cost him way too much.

Lee had known from the beginning that Jeremy was not a good fit for his church. He was young and unorthodox and dressed casually in Khaki pants or jeans even when he gave the sermon. He spoke of walking with God as if he were a personal friend. New Life was a comfortable church. Influential, professional people like him made up the congregation and leadership. They weren't interested in any of that radical "walking with Jesus" craziness Jeremy had plans to introduce. Lee needed the church for contacts, and it was good for his business to be a church leader. However, Brandon had nothing but praise for Jeremy. He said the church would benefit from the kind of inspiration Jeremy could give and that the church needed to be more "relevant," as he called it. He was sure Jeremy was the man to make it happen. In the end, Brandon had won over the church board, with only Lee and one other person objecting.

As he approached his driveway, he tried to calm himself. Now was not the time to explode. He had to be careful. Hopefully, Lisa wouldn't do or say anything idiotic. He couldn't afford to lose his temper with her now. Lee killed the engine and rubbed his hands over his face. Finally calm, he let himself in the house. Fortunately, Lisa was asleep on the couch. She wouldn't have a chance to bring him to fury tonight as she did so often these days.

CHAPTER SEVENTEEN

The sound of footsteps brought Vikki's eyes to her classroom door. It was Lisa's walk. She peered out the door and waved as Lisa came into view.

"Hi, Vikki," she greeted her, pausing at Vikki's door.

"Hi. How was your weekend?"

"Fine." After an awkward pause, Lisa continued. "Lee told me he saw you at church yesterday. I was home with a headache." She came in the door and lowered herself into the rocking chair at the reading center. With a nervous smile, she asked, "Did you come as someone's guest?"

Vikki crossed over to a table and perched on its edge. "Actually, I came with Jeremy, the associate pastor. He's a friend of mine."

"Oh. I see." Lisa stared at her lap and rocked in the chair a moment. She raised her head. "Listen, Vikki, I know you want to help me, but the best way to do that is to forget about what you heard and saw on Saturday." Her head shook slowly. "Lee won't let himself be dragged into any kind of scandal. You'll be the one to get hurt, and it won't help me at all."

Vikki raised her palms, "I don't know how to do that. How can I pretend nothing happened when I know Lee hits you?" She crossed her arms and hugged them close to her body. "He scared me at church, Lisa. It must be awful for you to live in that kind of fear."

Lisa's mouth quivered. "It's okay, Vikki," her voice cracked, and her eyes shadowed with the lie. "I've learned to cope. I can handle it."

Vikki walked to her and touched her shoulder. "Promise me you'll call if you need me. I'll come and get you. Call anytime, no matter how late. Do you understand? You don't have to live like this. All the money in the world can't be worth being beaten."

Lisa nodded and sniffed. "Thanks, Vikki. It means a lot to me." She smiled weakly. "Actually, Lee was unusually kind to me yesterday. Maybe seeing you at church caused him to think."

"Maybe," Vikki agreed, though her face revealed her doubt.

* * *

"Well, hello, Jessie." The male voice was unmistakable, chilling her to the bone.

"Lee?" Her face paled. What was he doing here? Surely, he didn't attend this church. She paused in her trek to the door. Jordan waited at her side. She gazed up at the tall man, and her hand flew to her mouth.

"I noticed you Sunday, but I don't believe you saw me." His smile was arrogant and intimidating.

Jessie fought the queasiness forming in the pit of her stomach. "No, I... I just started coming here. My... My brother is the associate pastor here. He invited me to this Wednesday Bible study group."

Lee's face was stone cold, and recognition flashed in his eyes. "I don't believe we've met," he offered as he turned to Jordan.

"Hi, I'm Jordan. Nice to meet you." He shot Jessie a confused look.

"I'm Lee Bannister, an elder here." Lee's haughty smile was still in place as he shook Jordan's hand. "Perhaps you'll find New Life Community Church to your liking."

"Thank you, I found tonight's Bible Study enjoyable." Jordan returned.

Lee nodded. "I'm sure I'll see you around, Jessie." Contempt oozed from his voice.

Jordan studied him as he walked away. He frowned. "Is your friend always so pleasant?"

Jessie's head was spinning, and she struggled against the urge to bolt out the door. She had believed he was out of her life for good. Why in the world would he be attending this church? And what a joke, he was an elder? "Oh, he's just a jerk," she said hoarsely, "I used to work for him a while back." She took Jordan's arm. "Let's go get a sandwich somewhere, okay?"

Jordan cocked his head. "Sure. Are you okay?"

"Yes, I just feel a little lightheaded, probably because I skipped supper. I need something to eat, that's all."

Jessie sat in the front seat, rubbing her hands together. Jordan pulled into the parking space at the restaurant and turned toward her. "What's the matter, Jessie? That guy really got to you, didn't he?"

Jessie looked at him and produced a weak smile. "Nothing, I'm fine. Let's go in."

Jordan watched as Jessie picked at her food. "You've hardly touched anything. Are you still feeling sick?"

"I'm feeling a little better, and I've eaten some of my sandwich." Jessie took another bite. "See." She smiled across the table at him. But her smile was uneasy.

After a quiet meal, Jordan drove to Jessie's apartment. He walked her to the door. He took her hands and turned her toward himself. "You look better now, but you seemed awfully upset about running into that guy at church. Do you want to tell me why he shook you up so much?"

Jessie pulled at her hands, but Jordan didn't release his grip. How could she possibly tell him the reason for her behavior? She forced an indifferent tone of voice. "I used to work in his law office as a file clerk. We had a falling out, so I quit." She presented the most reassuring face she could muster. "It's no big deal, okay? He just took me by surprise, that's all." Her eyes betrayed the words she spoke.

"Okay," Jordan shrugged. His expression was uneasy. "You were both kind of surprised, I think."

He hesitated at the entrance to Jessie's apartment. "Are you sure you are all right?"

"I'm sure. Don't worry about me." She kissed him lightly. "Bye, Jordan."

"Bye, Jessie." His eyes searched her face. "Get some rest, Love."

* * *

Late into the evening, Jessie was still trying to convince herself that running into Lee wasn't that big of a deal. She sat at her table sipping hot tea, hoping to calm the churning in her stomach. So what? Lee attended New Life Community. Jessie wasn't a regular there. She'd only been to a couple of services and a Bible study group. She never had to go back. Jordan would understand. She'd tell him the truth; she wasn't the church-going type. Besides, Lee wouldn't do anything to put himself in a compromising position. She was sure of that.

No, he would use any measures necessary to protect his position as an elder.

She thought back on the summer after her junior year of college when she worked as a file clerk for Smith and Whitley's law office. She was a cocky twenty-one-year-old, ready to challenge all her Christian parents had taught her. But it was that summer that she made the worst choice of her young life.

Mr. Lee Bannister was a charming and handsome lawyer at Smith and Whitley's, and one of the partners, Bryan Smith, was his father-in-law. Jessie soon learned that, though he was married, Mr. Bannister had an eye for the ladies. Rumors of affairs and plenty of flirting and teasing between Lee and the female employees were common.

Jessie's duties consisted of filing papers and occasional memo typing when the two secretaries were behind in their paperwork. She noticed that when Bryan Smith was out of the office, Lee often had her come to his office and type a letter for him. He insisted that his secretary had "a mountain of work to finish," so he needed her to help him out.

Jessie was quite willing to help her boss on these occasions because it flattered her ego to think he was attracted to her, and she enjoyed the flirting. Besides, Lee was tall and handsome with his chiseled jaw and dark hair that was beginning to gray at the temples. He was off-limits, of course, but it didn't hurt to participate in his little game. He wasn't her type anyway—too old and stuffy. She was unprepared, though, when one evening Lee asked her to work late with him.

Jessie cringed as the memories flooded through her being and shook her to the core.

Lee walked around the desk and touched her shoulder. "Why don't you let me buy you a drink before we go home? I sure could use one after this day." He chuckled. "Really, I don't know how we would have gotten it all done without your willingness to help." Taking a step closer, he turned to face her and took both her hands in his.

Surprised though she was, she could not deny that his boldness flattered her. "Sure, why not?" She hesitated, "As long as your wife won't mind."

Lee tilted his head back with a look of amusement. "I'm asking you for a drink, nothing more."

His remark and condescending look unsettled her. "Fine then. Let's go." She pulled her hands away, grabbed her bag, and started for the door.

"Wait, I just thought of something." Lee beamed with a self-satisfied smile. "I seem to remember I have a bottle of wine in the closet. It was left over from the Christmas party, and I was saving it for an occasion just like this. Since it is getting late, we could just have a drink to celebrate making it through the week and save the driving time." He raised one finger to make his point. "That way you won't be out too late. How about that?"

"Okay, but I really don't drink much."

"Just one little drink. We wouldn't want you to drive home intoxicated." He had taken her hand in his and now ran a finger along her arm.

To her shock, Lee stepped closer and drew her to him. His eyes had a look that Jessie could not misread. She tried to pull away, but he pulled her in, and his lips met hers. "Jessie, come here," he whispered as he led her to the couch in his office.

Startled, Jessie separated herself from him with a shove. "Lee, I want to go home." His actions were no longer innocent flirting.

Anger flared in Lee's eyes for just a second. "Come on, Jessie. You surely knew where this was leading. I don't think you're that innocent." His voice was sarcastic at the onset but then took on a silky tone. "I could fix it so that you had a full-time job here as my secretary if you play your cards right."

"Play my cards right?" Jessie's voice fumed with anger. "Sorry, but I don't have affairs with married men. Your wife is sitting home waiting for you while you come on to me. How dare you!" She picked up her bag and marched to the door.

With one fluid motion, Lee positioned himself in front of her. "Oh, come on. I'm sorry. I would never force anything on you." His voice was softer now, almost gentle. "Anyway, don't you know my wife left me. I thought everyone knew that. Our divorce was final last week." He stepped closer to her. "You and I would be perfect together. I've been waiting for this moment for a long time. You're gorgeous." He took her hands and brought them up to his lips. "Now that I'm free, we won't have anything to keep us from having a relationship."

Jessie studied him. Was he telling the truth, or was this just an attempt to seduce her? She had to admit she was attracted to him, and though he was at least fifteen years older than her, it was appealing to imagine being the girlfriend of a mature, sophisticated, man.

He kissed her again with more passion than before. She didn't fight it at all. For a moment, the teachings of her parents and church threatened to interfere, but she carelessly tossed them aside as she had done a few times before.

She was in turmoil as she drove home later that evening. What was wrong with her? She wasn't the type to sleep around. What if the whole thing was no big deal to Lee? She was probably just another notch on his belt. Now the rumors of his affairs rang all too true. But he did imply he wanted a relationship now that he was divorced.

Jessie's fears grew the following day. Lee distanced himself and barely spoke to her until late in the afternoon when he called her into his office to type a memo. He shut the door and turned to her. "Jessie," he said, sounding businesslike, "Last night was fun, but you know it was only that, fun, right? We might even get together again. I don't want you to think it was personal or anything."

His words stunned her. Even though she hadn't imagined he was in love with her, she had hoped he at least cared for her enough to pursue a relationship now that his marriage was over. "Oh, sure," she faked a smile, "I realize you'd want to take it slow since you just got divorced."

"My divorce? Oh, yeah. I did say that, didn't I? You really are naïve, aren't you?" he chuckled and sat in the chair behind his desk.

Feeling sick, she slid down in the chair facing Lee's desk. "You lied to me? You're not divorced. I only stayed because I thought you were interested in a relationship. I thought it meant something to you." A tear slid down her cheek.

He flashed a patronizing smile. "Oh, it did mean something to me. You are incredibly alluring, and I'd like to get together again. But surely you don't think I'd leave my wife over a little fling. I've got way too much at stake to ruin it over some one-night stand." His arm swept the room. "It's all mine when my wife's old man, Bryan Smith, retires. I'd be a fool to give that up now, wouldn't I?" His face mocked her. "Hmmm… I figured you were more experienced in these types of affairs. You need to grow up a little."

Jessie shook her head and took a sip of her now cold tea. Memories of her encounter with Lee brought back all the feelings of guilt she had buried. She knew it had been wrong. Her family and the church would say she should repent and ask for forgiveness. But what was the use? She had strayed too far from the Christian life to go back now. She poured out the rest of her tea and got ready for bed.

Maybe running into Lee tonight was all for the best. She

had given up the church deal a few years ago and only went last Sunday to please her brother. Jordan inviting her was the only reason she went to the Bible study, even though it had started to feel like this was a church she could support. She was sure Jordan was getting too serious about her anyway, and as charmed as she was when he proclaimed his love for her, she was sure it would never work out. Jordan was a good Christian man. He was looking for a different kind of girl. The next time they were together, she would tell him she just wasn't ready for a serious relationship.

* * *

Jordan's thoughts were so intent on Jessie and her strange reaction to Lee Bannister's appearance at church the night before he didn't hear Jeremy's approach and jumped at the sound of his voice.

"I'm sorry I startled you. You looked like you were a thousand miles away."

Realizing that he had been staring into space on the edge of his bunk with a broom in his hand, Jordan abruptly stood and started moving the broom over the fire station's tile floor. "Just sweeping up around here. Are you wanting to get some lunch?"

Jeremy peered at his friend. "It's only 10 o' clock, Bud. Don't you think that's a bit early?"

"Oh, I thought it was later." He continued to sweep the same area absentmindedly.

"Is something bothering you? Or are you just trying to make these few tiles especially clean?"

"Oh, right. I guess I have swept around here enough." He paused as if trying to decide whether to speak further. Just then, the alarm sounded, and both men rushed to prepare for the call.

. . .

It was a car wreck that needed their services. A woman and her child were injured while the other vehicle's intoxicated driver stumbled around until he was finally handcuffed and hauled into a squad car.

Jeremy assessed the little girl's injuries and determined they were not life-threatening. He bandaged a cut on her head and splinted her left arm that had sustained a break, all the while soothing her with soft, assuring words.

Jeremy then assisted his partner as he calmly and skillfully treated the mother, who was more seriously injured. Jordan started an IV after consulting with the doctor by phone and then positioned the woman and assisted in getting her into the ambulance.

Jeremy rode with the patient in the back while Jordan drove them to the hospital. He marveled at the way Jordan had become instantly aware and focused when the alarm had sounded, though he had seemed lost in another world just seconds before. He knew it was the mark of an experienced and talented paramedic, along with the adrenaline rush that filled every sense of a first responder's being.

After finishing paperwork and cleaning up, Jeremy smiled and said, "Now I'm ready for lunch. How about you?"

"Sure, where to?"

* * *

They drove to a nearby sandwich joint and ordered. The two men discussed the morning's events and the senseless accident due to drunk driving. During a pause in the conversation, Jordan brought his fist down on the table abruptly. "Now, I remember that guy's name."

"What guy?"

"Jeremy, do you know anybody by the name of Bannister at your church? I think his first name is Levi or something."

Jeremy was instantly alert. "There's a guy named Lee Bannister. He's an elder."

"That's it. Do you know any reason it would be upsetting for Jessie to run into him?"

"No, why?" Jeremy asked, taking a bite of his sandwich.

"Well, he approached Jessie as we were leaving Bible study yesterday, and it really shook her up. He was super arrogant and snobbish in the way he spoke to her."

Jeremy looked baffled. "I didn't even know they knew each other."

"She only said she had worked for him and they'd had some kind of disagreement. She apparently quit the job because of it."

Jeremy frowned. How strange. Why had Lee's name come up again, and why in the world would his presence upset Jessie? He brushed his hand across his forehead. "I don't know. I had no idea they had any connections."

"Oh, well. It was probably just an awkward situation for both of them." Jordan finished his soda. "He sure wasn't friendly at all, even though he approached her."

What kind of guy was this Lee anyway? Jeremy mused. Vikki was sure he beat his wife, and now he had caused both her and Jessie distress after meeting at church. It was just too strange.

CHAPTER EIGHTEEN

Jessie's phone started ringing as she put the key in the door to her apartment. She fumbled around in her purse and grabbed it. "Hello," she said louder than she meant.

"Hi, did you just get home?"

"Hi, Jordan. Yeah, I was trying to open my door and find my phone at the same time."

"Oh sorry. Do you want to call me back later?"

"No, it's fine. I can talk now."

"Well, I just wanted to know if you would like to go out to dinner and maybe catch a movie."

She paused. "I'm really tired, Jordan. I'm not sure I'm up to being out late."

"Well, we could just go get something to eat and make it an early evening."

She almost declined the date but had another thought. She did need to talk to Jordan, and the conversation would only be more difficult if she put it off. "That sounds good to me."

While talking at the local pizza place, Jessie noticed

how Jordan's eyes shone with interest as she spoke, an attitude so different from that of men she usually dated. He seemed engaged in the conversation. It made her wish she was another type of girl—one who had values she knew the man seated across the table would expect in a girlfriend. He had said as much at the park the other day. All he cared about was that she was a Christian. Not that she wasn't. She did believe, after all. It was the hypocrisy from some Christians she knew that turned her off. Besides, she hadn't been living a Christian life.

It didn't matter anyway. Jessie knew she would have to tell Jordan about her past—especially her connection to Lee. It would be heartless to end the relationship without explanation. Jordan was a good guy who deserved better. She couldn't let him assume something that wasn't true about her. Even so, Jessie wished it could be different. She could so easily fall for his charm and good looks, but she couldn't erase her past mistakes. She let out a soft sigh.

"I'm sorry." Jordan looked at her with concern. "I've kept you out longer than I should have. I know you're tired."

"No, it's okay, really. I just sort of drifted. I'm sorry. I really am having a nice time."

Jordan's face was intense. "Let's get you home. You look beat."

Their conversation was enjoyable on the way home, and Jessie couldn't bring herself to spoil the mood. When Jordan walked her to the door, she invited him in. She would tell him over a cup of coffee.

"Are you sure? I don't want to keep you up."

"I want to talk to you for a few minutes," she said.

"Okay, I won't pass up an opportunity to spend time with you."

"Do you like iced coffee? I found a delicious recipe."

Jordan raised his eyebrows, and his eyes twinkled. "I'm game. I've never tried iced coffee."

"Well, you don't know what you're missing. You can find some glasses in the cabinet by the refrigerator."

Jordan placed the glasses on the table and watched as Jessie made the coffee and took a jar from the refrigerator.

"I made a batch of syrup yesterday. It's good for several servings."

Jordan swiped his finger around the edge of the jar. "Mmm. That's good."

Jessie gave his hand a playful smack. "Stop, you're like a little kid." she teased.

Jordan grinned. "Yes, Ma'am." He took a sip of the coffee. "This is good stuff."

"I thought you would like it. We can sit on the couch in the great room."

After a few minutes, Jessie turned and met Jordan's gaze. He leaned over and lightly brushed her lips with a kiss. Jessie looked at him with sorrowful eyes then turned away.

"Jessie, what's wrong?" His voice was gentle, and he eased her around to face him. She was a portrait of regret.

Jessie scooted a few inches away, needing the distance. "We need to talk," she whispered.

"Okay." He waited, afraid of what she might say. It always seemed to end this way.

"Jordan," her eyes met his, and she could barely ask the question, "Have you ever?" she paused, fighting for words.

His eyes rounded, but he didn't interrupt, sensing her struggle to voice the question.

She took a deep breath, "I know guys like you don't... I mean... usually don't, have you been with... been in a relationship with a woman?" Her voice was barely audible.

He moved his head a little, and his mouth opened. "Um, are you asking me if I've ever slept with a girl?"

"Yes," she whispered. Her eyes fell to her lap.

He might have been amused at the situation, except she seemed so troubled. He lifted her chin and looked into her eyes, "No..." he shook his head. "I haven't." He wasn't sure that was the answer she wanted to hear, but he continued slowly. "I made a promise to God a long time ago to wait until marriage, and... with His help, I've, uh, managed to keep it," his head tilted slightly, a trace of mischief on his face, "so far."

Anxiety and sadness mingled on Jessie's face. Jordan lightly squeezed her hands.

"Talk to me," he said softly.

"I'm not the girl for you, Jordan." Her eyes snapped in sudden defensiveness. "I'm, I'm not a virgin." She searched his face for disgust or shock but saw only compassion. Those emotions would have been easier for her to handle. She went on, "I've had more than one relationship. I'm sorry, but I am sure I don't make your list for the perfect woman." Her eyes spilled, and she angrily swiped her tears. She knew it was over.

Jordan took her face in his hands, "Okay, so you've made choices I haven't made," he said carefully, "We all have plenty of regrets and sins to answer for." There was no hint of judgment in his tone.

Confusion played on her face. "But, I thought all Christian men wanted a virgin bride, especially if—if they'd waited themselves."

He drew her in even closer and peered into her very soul, willing her to understand. "It's not about me, Jessie, or what I want. I made my promise to God, not because I had expectations about my future wife, but because I believed it was the right thing to do." He paused, "Sure, I wish you had waited, but not for my benefit. I just believe that it's God's best plan for us." His eyes locked on hers. "What you've done in the past doesn't matter to me. That's between you and God. I only care about who you are now. And He is the only one you need forgiveness from. All you have to do is ask." Hot tears spilled from her eyes as he reached for her and held her close. "I love you, Jessie," he whispered.

Jordan rose from the couch, "Here, let me get you a Kleenex." He walked to the bathroom to get the box, brought it to Jessie, and sat down close to her.

Jessie took the offered Kleenex, wiped her eyes, and then snuggled up to Jordan. She was quiet, attempting to sort out her emotions. One thing was undeniable, Jessie had never met a man like him before. He loved her for the person she was. She knew something else; she was falling for him, and she had no resources to fight it.

Jordan's lips met hers in a gentle kiss, and she caressed his cheek with her fingers. He pulled her down on the couch and kissed her again. His fingers ran through her hair and along the side of her sweater. Longing pulsed through his veins; he had never felt such a connection with any girl in his life.

An alarm emerging deep within his soul jolted him. He had to cool this now, or he would be powerless to control it. He forced himself away from her and sat up. "Jessie, I think I should probably leave now."

She sat up as he did. "I'm sorry, Jordan."

"Don't be sorry." He looked at her in awe. He had never been closer to breaking his vow. "I want to be with you, Jessie," he breathed, "but not now, not like this. I think I should go home."

"Please don't leave yet." She stood and stepped a few feet away. "There's something else I need to tell you. Could we go to the table and talk? I'll sit across from you."

He couldn't stifle a grin. "I don't know Jessie, I can probably reach you across the table."

She almost laughed, but the giggle caught in her throat.

"It's important that I tell you something. It may change your mind about me after all."

He shook his head, his eyes dusky with feeling. "I doubt it."

They walked to the table, and Jessie seated herself across from him as she had promised. Jordan stood up and walked to her refrigerator, still reeling with the intensity of the moment. "I need something to drink. My throat is dry. Too bad I'm not a drinking man." He snickered and pulled out a can of soda. " I guess this will have to do. Do you want anything?"

"I'm fine, thanks."

"Okay, so what's so awful that you think might drive me away?" he flirted, beginning to feel in control again. He sat down in the chair on the other side of the table.

"I'm serious, Jordan. Did you know how upset I was when I met Lee at church?"

"Yeah, I have been wondering about that."

"Remember, I told you that I worked for him?" He nodded. "Well, we worked alone late one night and I—I made a terrible mistake." She paused and bit her lower lip.

"Oh, Jessie."

"It was a one-time thing, and he lied to me about being divorced." The ugliness of it all infused her entire being as it did every time she remembered. She recounted the awful night, revealing only the necessary details, including how Lee had treated her the next day and how their encounter meant nothing to him. "He wasn't even planning to get divorced. It was all a lie," she choked out.

When her story ended, she looked sick with guilt. "I'm not that way, Jordan. I'd never had an affair with a married man before and wouldn't have if I had known the truth then. And I've never been the promiscuous type."

Jordan's eyes had not strayed from her face as she spoke.

"Well, now I understand why seeing him upset you so much." He was at a loss for words to comfort her, so he sat without speaking as she wept. He crossed to the seat beside her and put his arm around her shoulders, giving her a gentle squeeze.

"That's not all," she sniffed. "I was so angry, I found his number and called his wife."

"You did?" Jordan's mouth fell open. "What did she say?"

"I'm not sure she believed me. At least, she didn't want to. I told myself I was telling her for her own good, but later I realized I wanted to lash out at Lee, to destroy his marriage and his chance to own the law office."

"Does she know who you are?"

"I don't think so. I think I told her my first name, but we've never met. I can't go back to that church, Jordan. It would only cause trouble for Lee's wife and Jeremy. Lee won't let anyone or anything interfere with his plans to own the law office one day. He will guard his reputation at all costs." Jessie shifted in her seat and met Jordan's eyes. "Jeremy has no idea I know Lee. I don't want to hurt anybody, and I have never told anybody else about this."

But Jeremy did know his sister had connections with Lee, Jordan realized, remembering his conversation with him. "I can't believe that scumbag could be an elder," he said.

"But Jordan, he didn't force me. I could have said no."

"He was in a position of authority over you, he lied, and he intimidated you. Besides, he's married and in a leadership position at church." He paused for a moment then continued. "I suppose we could find another church, even though I can't imagine Lee bringing the subject up. He wouldn't be that stupid." Jordan studied his can of Coke. "The only problem would be if his wife did remember your name and figured out who you were. And you would always be uncomfortable there."

Jessie stared at a picture on the kitchen wall. "I'll understand if you want to end our relationship, Jordan. I'm sure it's more than you bargained for." She looked back at him with tear-filled eyes.

Jordan was taken aback a little by all she had confessed, no question about it, but her vulnerability only caused him to love her more. She had trusted him with her darkest secrets. He stood, raised her from her chair, and embraced her. "I'm not your judge. I love you. I love your honesty and how you trust me with your heart. I will never betray that trust." He held her close, gave her a slow, sweet kiss, and felt himself drifting into her amber eyes. "I really do need to leave, Jessie. I wouldn't want to hate myself in the morning," he quipped, easing the intensity of the moment.

"Okay," she sighed, "all this has worn me out anyway."

He kissed her on the cheek. "Goodbye, Love," he said softly and walked out the door.

* * *

Jeremy was working late Friday evening on his message. It was his third Sunday to speak, and he felt more comfortable on each occasion. He was distracted by Jordan's comments earlier in the day. Why *would* seeing Lee Bannister upset Jessie? What could have happened at work that could shake her up so much?

And what was with this Lee character? He let his thoughts wander to earlier this afternoon when Vikki had come home from work. Vikki had pulled in the drive right behind him. He stood by his car and waited for her. Watching her stride toward him, seeing her smile, gave him the warm feeling you get when you see your best friend. He was glad it had worked out this way. Their friendship had flourished despite his misguided actions that night a few weeks ago.

"Hi, how was work?"

She smiled. "Okay, I guess. How was your day?"

"Ok," he worked at Heather's car seat strap and pulled her from the car. He placed her on the ground, and she trotted off to the front porch, her golden curls bouncing around her head. "It was busy. We had an accident caused by some drunk, but though the injuries were serious, they weren't life-threatening."

Vikki's green eyes were bright in the afternoon sun. Sometimes they were more golden, but today they were almost a jade color. "Well, I hope they take that drunk driver's license away," she snapped, her eyes flared with the words.

"They probably will, at least for a while." He walked her to the porch. "Can we sit and talk for a few minutes?'

"Sure, would you like something to drink?"

"No, I'm fine." They settled in the wicker chairs. "I've been thinking about Lee Banister." He leaned forward, his elbows in his lap. "How was Lisa this week anyway? Heather shuffled up to him and raised her hands. He scooped her up, sat her on his lap, and gave her a box of animal crackers he'd grabbed from the car.

Vikki considered the question. "We only talked seriously on Monday morning. She said Lee saw me at church, and she warned me about getting involved. Basically, she let me know I should stay out of it. She told me things had been better over the weekend, but I think I noticed a new bruise on her arm today." She shook her head. "I'm sure she is being abused, but I don't know what to do." Her fingers found her cross necklace.

"Somehow, he's got my sister worked up, too. Jordan told me Lee approached Jessie at church Wednesday. Apparently, he was pretty intimidating to her. She told Jordan that she used to work for Lee and quit over some falling out. But he thinks there's more to it than that."

"Maybe she's afraid of him. I know he frightened me at church." She clenched her fists, and her voice tensed. "I'm telling you, he beats his wife and has her scared to death, and I'm not doing anything about it. What kind of person am I?"

"What can you do?" Jeremy sat Heather near a basket of toys Vikki kept on her porch and scooted his chair closer. He put his hands on Vikki's knees. "Vikki, I know you feel helpless, but until she is ready to admit she needs help, you can't do anything. I'll help her if she wants me to. I can bring her here, or take her to a shelter, but she has to be ready to accept help."

"Would you talk to her? I mean come to school after the kids leave one day."

Jeremy hesitated. "I don't know if she would want me to intervene without permission."

"What if I asked her? Would you come?"

"I'll come, but only if she agrees."

She smiled and squeezed his hands. "Thank you. At least I won't be guilty of doing nothing. We are going to work on some plans together tomorrow. Maybe I'll ask her then."

He gave her a half-smile and shook his head. "Somehow I can't say no to you."

She smiled then, her emerald eyes wide and innocent.

They conversed a few minutes more, and then Jeremy excused himself to work on his message. He gathered Heather, and the three went into the house. He paused at the door leading up to his apartment. "Maybe we can play cards with Jordan and Jessie tomorrow if I get finished with my sermon tonight."

"Sounds fun. I'll see you tomorrow." She looked into his face. "Thank you for trying to help." On an impulse, she lifted her head and kissed his cheek.

An inkling of a smile played on his face and he ran his fingers through his hair.

"I'm sorry, Jeremy," she whispered, her cheeks reddening.

"Oh, don't be sorry." He leaned back against the door-frame. "I kinda liked it." With those words, he smiled roguishly and darted up the steps with Heather trailing behind.

Heather's stirring pulled him out of his daydream. She had fallen asleep on the couch while he worked. He strolled over and picked her up. "Come on, Angel. Let's get you to bed." He carried her to her bed and tucked her in. Bending down, he brushed her hair away from her eyes. "Thank you, God, for giving me such a beautiful gift."

* * *

It was late when Vikki finally finished her plans for the next week. Like Jeremy, she wanted to have her weekend free. She was pleased that he had suggested playing cards with Jordan and Jessie. They were fun to be around, and it was apparent that Jordan was crazy about Jessie.

Vikki tried to believe she was content with the way things were between Jeremy and herself. They had become good friends, and that was fine. But she knew she was lying to herself. She wanted more than friendship. She had fallen in love with Jeremy the night he kissed her on his balcony and told her the story about Shannon. Sometimes, Vikki thought she saw him looking at her the same way he did the night he kissed her, but she was never sure if it was longing or loneliness she saw in his expression. With a sigh, she knelt by her bed to pray. "Dear God, please help Jeremy learn to love again." She paused, fighting against the words as she spoke them, "even if it's not me."

* * *

The jingling jarred Jessie out of deep sleep. Her alarm clock lit up with 2:05 in red digits. A feeling of dread consumed her. Something was wrong when people called at this hour. She stumbled to the table where her phone was charging.

"Hello," she stammered.

The answer was low, menacing, and the words were a bit slurred. "You won't go back to New Life Community Church if you know what's good for you."

Her blood ran cold, and she sank to the floor as she recognized Lee's voice. Why would he call her? And why at this hour? She wondered if he had been drinking.

"Hey! Do you hear me?" he barked.

Anger momentarily surpassed her fear. "What's the matter with you? You can't tell me what to do."

"Stay away from the church, Jessie. I don't need my wife to make any connections. I know you called her four years ago and told her about our little affair. I convinced her then that you were just some disgruntled employee that I'd had to fire, but I can't take any chances."

"Maybe you should have thought about that then," Jessie accused. "The way I see it, you're the one who needs to leave the church. After all, you're the elder. I'm just a poor little file clerk who was seduced by a church leader." Truthfully, he had unnerved her, but to her benefit, he couldn't see her trembling hands. "Nobody will care about me when they have an elder to crucify."

His laugh was wicked, and he cursed into the phone. "Who would believe that story? Especially since you just happen to be the new preacher's sister, and I just happen to be in a position with power to influence the board on his retention. Even if you told Jeremy everything, I could easily convince them that your brother made the whole story up to get me out of the eldership for some reason, and then he'd be the loser."

"Back off, Lee. You don't scare me," she lied.

His tone grew more threatening. "I'm warning you. Stay away from my church, and don't ever tell anyone you know me. Don't even consider exposing our little affair. I'll make sure you and your brother both suffer if you do. I'm going to be keeping an eye on you." He paused for a moment. "Oh, and I'm not above physical persuasion, if you know what I mean."

Prickles of fear ran down her arms. "Leave me alone," Jessie screamed into the phone and disconnected the call. She wasn't aware of how long she had been sitting on the floor until she realized she was shivering. The digits now shone 2:45. She crept back to bed and sank deep in the covers where sleep eluded her while the clock named the hours. It was five in the morning before her eyes closed into a fitful sleep.

CHAPTER NINETEEN

Not finding Lisa's car around the front, Vikki drove to the east end of the building, parked her car, and jogged up the stairs to her classroom. As she leaned over the table, sorting through the stack of space posters, she heard the click of footsteps making their way to her end of the hall.

"Hi, Vikki, I guess I should have parked at this end of the building. I'm just used to coming in the front door."

Still standing with her back to the door, Vikki greeted her friend. "Hi, Lisa, I thought I'd go ahead and get these posters out. I was thinking of grouping the students in pairs and having them make a poster report to present in class."

"Hey, what do you think about pairing students from your class with my students?" Lisa suggested. "It might be a nice change for the kids."

"Sounds good to me." Vikki straightened, turned toward Lisa for the first time, and caught her breath. "What happened to your arm?"

"Oh, it was crazy. I'm such a klutz sometimes. I fell down

the stairs and broke my arm." Lisa tapped the cast. "At least it's my left arm. Can you believe that?

"No," Vikki shook her head. "I can't believe it at all."

"Well, it's true," Lisa protested, her smile vanishing. She turned away in a huff. "Maybe today isn't a good day to work together. I'll just work on it myself."

"No, don't go," Vikki touched Lisa's good arm. "Come on," she pleaded. "Let's work on this project."

Lisa faced Vikki and sighed. "Well, okay. I guess we can."

Palpable tension hung in the air as the teachers worked, and they spoke only when necessary. The strained atmosphere ebbed after a while, allowing for guarded conversation. After deciding how to pair the children and the guidelines for the project, they began constructing the bulletin board. Lisa's cast didn't allow for much help in cutting or stapling, but she could hand the pieces to Vikki and critique the visual effect. Lisa stepped back to appraise their labors. "It looks nice to me. What do you think?"

"Pretty good," Vikki replied. She stretched her arms. "I'm getting hungry. Do you have time to get something to eat?

Lisa straightened a couple of letters on the bulletin board. "Why don't you go get some sandwiches?" She looked at the clock above the door. "I can stay for a while. I'll finish up here and then do a few things in my room until you get back."

"That's fine." Vikki hesitated, choosing her words with care. "Lisa," she paused, "Lisa, would you talk to Jeremy? Maybe he could help somehow. He said he would be willing if you agreed."

Lisa wheeled around; her features were stony, "I told you, Vikki, stay out of this. I fell down the stairs, okay? End of story."

"But it's not the end. Were you running from Lee, or did he just push you down the stairs?" Vikki bit out.

"Stay out of this, Vikki. I can handle it."

Vikki reached for her purse that she had tossed on one of the desks. She dug through it for a minute then produced a flyer. "Look, I found this in the church restroom. It's a pamphlet about a shelter for women."

Lisa stared at the leaflet and shook her head. Her expression softened. "I don't think that will help me. I could never go to a shelter."

"Why not?" She thrust it toward her friend. "At least read it. It has the information you might need to know. The people there can offer counseling and shelter for you and your daughter if need be." Her eyes pleaded. "Please take it."

Lisa accepted the offered brochure and placed it on top of her book bag. "I'll read through it, okay?" She touched Vikki's arm. "Thanks for trying to help, but there's nothing you can do. Just stay out of it."

Vikki wrote down Lisa's choice and drove to Wendy's. Lisa was wrong about one thing. There was something she could do. Jeremy had told her about his disappointing visit with Brandon. She could go to Brandon herself and advise him about the broken arm before Lee had the chance to offer his lies. But would she be brave enough? Would Brandon believe her story?

As she pulled back into the school lot with the sandwiches, she drew in a deep breath. Lee's black BMW sat near the front door. Dreading what might be happening inside the building, she drove to the east end where she had parked earlier. Vikki sat in her car for a few minutes, afraid of what she might walk in on if she went into the building. Vikki climbed out of her car and walked to the door. As she crept up the stairs, loud voices confirmed her fears.

"Where have you been?" Lee bellowed in a fury. "I tried calling you, but you didn't answer."

Vikki peeked around the corner and saw Lee's frame outside Lisa's doorway. Anger contorted his face. She stepped around the corner and inched closer, no longer caring if Lee saw her.

Lisa noticed Vikki but looked away as she spoke to her husband. "I've been right here Lee, calm down. I was working with Vikki in her room and left my phone on my desk. When you first got here, I was in the workroom using the die cutter to make letters." Her tone was gentle and urgent as if she was trying to soothe a child throwing a tantrum. Her hands trembled. "I should have called. I'm sorry."

Scorn filled his face, and his clenched knuckles were white. "You're sorry and you think that makes it all right," Lee sneered. "I was called to an important meeting, and I couldn't go because you left Jennifer for me to watch. Then I come looking for you," his hands were flailing, "and you're not even where you are supposed to be!" He shoved his wife, and she crumpled to the floor.

Vikki hadn't noticed the weeping little girl cowered against the closet doors until he spoke the child's name. She wanted to shout at the brute, but only a whispered screech escaped her mouth.

Lee spun around at the sound and paled at the sight of Vikki. Panic flitted across his features as he drew close to her face, "Stay away from my wife you nosey little witch," he roared. He grabbed up the back of Lisa's hair, pulled her to her feet, and hauled her to where Vikki stood frozen with fright. "And don't spill your guts to your boyfriend or you won't even recognize her on Monday." He tugged his wife's hair causing her to yelp. "Tell her, Lisa," he growled.

"Vikki," she begged, tears flowing down her face, "Don't say anything about this, please. It will be better for me, I swear. He won't hurt me if you keep quiet."

"That's right. You keep your mouth shut, and I won't touch her. You'll see for yourself tomorrow at church. But," his eyes narrowed to slits, "if anyone hears of this, she'll suffer for it, and so will you! I am not about to lose everything over your meddling!" He released his grip on his wife and sprang at Vikki. Trapping her with his arms on either side of her body, he held her against the wall. The food and drinks flew from her arms. "And," he smiled maliciously, his hot breath searing her senses, "I have enough influence with the church board to destroy that preacher boyfriend of yours and his slut of a sister." He backed away and jerked the pamphlet about the women's shelter from his jacket pocket. "Lisa won't be needing this," he smirked as he ripped it in half and threw it on the floor. Vikki sagged against the wall, paralyzed with rage and terror,

"You'll be sorry for this," she breathed, instantly wishing she could take back the words.

"It would be very unwise for you to call anyone," his voice raised, "or tell anyone, especially Jeremy, what you've seen." He swung his hand close to her cheek, then curled his lips in a vicious smile. "Do you understand me?" Vikki gaped at him with dread, unable to speak. "Do you understand me?" he repeated, thrusting his face within inches of hers.

"Yes," she choked out, her eyes wide with terror.

"Good, because I'll be watching you." He backed away and looked at Lisa. "Go home! I'll be there for supper," he bellowed to his wife, then stomped down the hall.

Lisa gestured to her little daughter, still crouched sobbing by the closet doors. "Come on, Jennifer, it's okay, now." The dark-haired little girl looked at her mother with huge eyes. The fear emanating from them broke Vikki's heart. Lisa turned her tear-streaked face to Vikki, who had gotten back on her feet, "I'm so sorry," she sobbed, "Please don't say anything." Lisa put her arm around her daughter, and they hobbled down the hall, leaving Vikki rooted to the floor.

Vikki watched in stunned silence as Lisa and her daughter walked away. She melted to the floor, buried her head in her hands, and sobbed. Several minutes later, she stood with wobbly legs and walked to the restroom for paper towels so she could begin the cleanup of spilled drinks and food.

Her hands were still shaky when she finished the chore, but she made it down the stairs and to her car where she tried to process the morning's events and what her response should be. She could no longer consult Jeremy, not after Lee's threat. And what in the world did he mean by that remark about Jeremy's sister? Full of unresolved questions, she pulled out of the parking lot and began her drive home.

Jeremy stopped raking and waved as Vikki's car pulled in the driveway. Heather gleefully jumped in the pile of leaves. "Hi, how are you doing?"

Vikki waved halfheartedly and hurried on toward the porch. She knew she wouldn't be able to talk without breaking down, and she definitely couldn't tell Jeremy anything—at least not now. She needed time to sort things out.

"Hey, what's wrong?" He caught up with her and stopped her with a hand on her shoulder. "Have you been crying?"

Her expression was defiant to keep tears from flowing. "No, I'm fine. I just have a cold." She twisted out of his touch. "I can't talk right now. I'm sorry, I'll see you later."

"Fine, then, forgive me for caring," he muttered as he stalked off and continued raking the leaves.

* * *

Vikki grabbed her phone. "Hello, Jordan."

"Hi, Vikki. Are we still on for cards? I haven't been able to reach Jessie to ask her, but I'll keep trying."

"Oh yeah," she paused. "I forgot all about that, um, but sure. Do you want to come over around 6:30, maybe order pizza?"

"Great, I'll keep trying to get a hold of Jessie."

Vikki peeked out the window. Jeremy was still raking, and her front yard was nearly clear of leaves. She opened her door and started toward him.

Jeremy caught her eye, but he looked away and kept raking. She stood quietly watching him. "Do you need something?" he asked without looking her way.

"Yes, I need to apologize," came her soft reply. "I'm sorry I was short with you when I came home." A pink blush rose on her cheeks.

He leaned on his rake and eyed her, stirred by her woeful expression. What was this power she had over him?

"I didn't mean to snub you. I was upset about something that happened at school this morning, and I couldn't talk right then. I'm sorry." She glanced around the yard. "Thanks for raking. You didn't have to." Her lips turned up in a slight smile, "You sure were raking those leaves like there was no tomorrow."

"Oh, just trying to keep up with Heather." He pointed to his daughter rolling around in a leaf pile and did his best to look put out. It was hopeless.

"By the way, do you remember we're playing cards tonight?" Vikki asked.

"Sure, I'm planning on it." Jeremy knew by her expression that something was wrong. He had never seen that haunted look in her eyes before. "Are you okay?"

"I'm fine, just a little tired, I guess."

"Care to talk about it?"

"I really can't right now. I've got to go." She spun around and headed inside.

Jeremy continued raking. He told himself it was probably nothing, just the stress of teaching, but he doubted that thought. Something more was troubling her.

CHAPTER TWENTY

After wandering around the mall, spending time flipping through books at the library, and visiting the coffee shop, all the while looking over her shoulder for Lee, Jessie had run out of places to go. This whole thing was crazy; she couldn't hide forever. She would find something else to do for a few hours and then go home. He had probably been drinking anyway and wouldn't even remember calling her. Her phone showed a missed call. She checked it, and to her relief, it was a voice message from Jordan.

Give me a call when you get a chance.

Jessie drove around until she noticed a theater. A movie, that was it. She got in line to purchase a few more hours of reprieve. Maybe after the movie she would trust her voice to call Jordan.

Coming out of the theater two hours later, Jessie looked at her phone—three more messages, all from Jordan. She released a long deep breath feeling a little foolish hiding out all day. Lee had just been trying to scare her, and he had

succeeded. She was spooked, that's all. She picked up the
phone and clicked Jordan's name.

* * *

Vikki glanced around at the group gathered in her living
room and decided to offer up her sister's idea. She wouldn't
be able to concentrate on a card game anyway.

"Hey, guys, how would you like to go to a benefit concert
for a child with leukemia tonight instead of playing cards?
My sister called a few minutes ago. This guy she's been
dating is the lead singer of one of the bands that will be playing. A farmer offered some land for the event. Mary said they
had several areas marked off for people who wanted to build
a small fire, and I have a couple of old blankets we could take
to sit on."

"What kind of music do they play?" Jordan asked.

"Mostly classic rock, some new stuff, and also a little bit
of contemporary Christian. Robbie, my sister's boyfriend,
recently became a believer."

"Sounds okay to me. What do you think, Jess?" Jeremy
asked his sister.

"I'm interested. Let's try it. We can always leave if we
want to."

Jeremy's mother had agreed to watch Heather during the
card game, so he phoned to inform her of the new plan.
"Well, let's go," he said as he finished the call.

"I'll drive," Jordan offered, and they all piled into his blue
Ford pickup. The event was only a few miles away, located in
a large grassy field. Several vendors had erected stands
bordering the perimeter offering drinks, hotdogs, and T-
shirts for sale. There were booths displaying pamphlets with
facts about childhood leukemia scattered around the venue.
Signs posted in various places stated that all profits went to

pay the child's medical expenses. A wooden stage sprawled on one edge of the pasture with speakers placed on either side. Fires burned in several designated fire pits, making the cool late October night comfortable jacket weather. Classic rock by Journey floated in the air. Several bands, including the one led by Robbie, were scheduled to play during the night.

The four of them wandered around and found a firepit near the back of the field, complete with three logs in the center. They gathered twigs and dry grass. Soon a cozy fire warmed the chilly air. Vikki unfolded the blankets she had brought and laid them around the fire. Mary and a tall young man wandered up to them. "Hi, Vikki, you remember Robbie."

Vikki smiled and nodded. "How are you doing, Robbie?"

"I'm good," he replied with a smile.

Vikki introduced him to the others and invited Mary and Robbie to join them at their fire. They made a cute couple. Mary was small and petite with long brown curls and big brown doe-like eyes, while Robbie was tall with wavy chin-length dark blond hair and rugged good looks. He had his arm draped loosely around Mary's shoulder, and she snuggled up against his side. Vikki was happy for her sister. She just wished she had someone like Robbie in her life.

"Does your band perform often?" Jordan asked the musician.

"Oh, about twice a month, usually at the Lakeside Bar and Grill, but we're looking for some better places. It can get a little unruly there." He smiled and squeezed Mary's hand, "We're looking for a different kind of atmosphere now."

Jeremy turned toward him. "Vikki said you are a new Christian."

"Yes, fairly. Mary started dragging me to her church," he said, grinning at Mary, "and what the minister said made a lot of sense. It's a little too formal for me, though. We're kind of looking around, trying different churches."

"You should visit New Life Community, where Jeremy preaches," Jordan offered, "It's not *too* straightlaced," he said with a wink.

Robbie wore a look of surprise. The guy sitting there in frayed jeans and hoodie with wavy hair that grazed his ears didn't seem the type. "You're a preacher?"

"Yeah," Jeremy smiled at him. "Does that seem so improbable?"

"Well, no, you just don't look like any preacher I've seen before. But, hey, that's cool. Maybe we'll check out your church."

"Hey, Preacher, maybe Robbie's band could play during the service. New Life could use a little 'new life' where the music is concerned. Those praise songs could use a little jazzin' up, don't you think?" Jordan kidded.

Jeremy laughed. "I agree, but I'm not sure the church is ready for a rock band." He looked at Robbie. "But maybe you guys could set up a concert on a Wednesday or Sunday evening."

"That sounds like an awesome idea. Hey, I gotta go now," Robbie said, looking at his phone. "We're up in about twenty minutes."

Mary went with him to help set up while the others hung around the fire. The girls were quiet, each one lost in thought.

Jordan stood up and yawned. "Well, this is certainly exciting," he scoffed. "We've gotta liven things up a bit."

Spotting some empty beer cans a few feet away, he grabbed them up. "Here. this one's on me," he laughed and tossed it to his unsuspecting friend.

"What are you up to?" Jeremy asked as he caught the can. What the heck? He'd play along. He raised the empty can to the sky and jumped to his feet, gesturing toward Jordan. "Let's party!"

Jordan doubled over with laughter at the girls' shocked expressions. "Whoa, now, Preacher Boy. Vikki, you'd better watch out. You never know what will happen when these angelic types cut loose!"

Jeremy's eyes held merriment as he gave Vikki a side glance, "He's right, you know." Sprinting over, he pulled her to her feet and twirled her around, dancing to the beat of the music.

"Come on, Preacher, you can do better than that," Jordan said as he pulled Jessie close, kissing her cheek.

Jeremy plopped on the grass, pulling Vikki down with him. "I've got you now," he teased.

"Oh yeah." She wrestled and thrashed around, flailing her hands and legs until he surrendered in tears of laughter. She climbed on his chest and held his hands up over his head.

"Okay, okay, I give up," Jeremy laughed. "You're a feisty little thing." He peered up at her with amusement.

Vikki tilted her chin. "I always end up on top," she said with a smug look.

Jeremy raised his eyebrows, "Is that so?" He shot her an impish grin. Vikki's eyes widened as color crept up her cheeks, and she quickly scrambled to her feet.

The four friends continued their antics for a few minutes more, then Jeremy picked up the beer cans and went looking for a trash barrel. He spied one near a wooded area and jogged over to it. A rustling within the trees drew his eyes, and he had a creepy feeling he was not alone. There was another rustle and then the sound of a stick cracking. A tingling sensation made his skin crawl. Was someone there? He scanned the tree line, but nothing was visible. It probably was a raccoon or opossum.

Jeremy strolled back to the group. He decided against

mentioning the noise he heard since it was most likely nothing to cause alarm. The friends talked and listened to Robbie's band for a while longer until Jeremy decided that they needed to leave soon to pick up Heather.

Jordan dropped Jeremy and Vikki off at the farmhouse. Jeremy invited Vikki to accompany him to get Heather, and with a look of surprise, she agreed. Jeremy tried with little luck to engage Vikki in conversation on the drive to his parents' house. She had been distracted most of the evening, and even when she'd played around at the fire, the haunted look had never completely left her eyes.

Heather spied Vikki when the door opened and ran to her for a hug. Vikki embraced the enthusiastic little girl. "Hi, Heather. Did you have a good time with your grandma and grandpa?" she asked and quickly released her.

Jeremy's mom gave Vikki a curious glance and then looked at her son. "I don't believe I've met your friend, have I?"

"Oh, I'm sorry. Mom and Dad, this is my friend Vikki. Vikki, these are my parents, Frank and Marianne."

Marianne greeted her, "Nice to meet you. Do you live around here?"

Before she could answer, recognition flashed across Frank's features. "I remember you. Aren't you Jeremy's land-lady? I thought at the time you were awfully young to own such a big place."

"Yes," Vikki voiced softly, her fingers on the cross that dangled from her neck. She turned to Jeremy's mother. "It's nice meeting both of you."

"Call me Marianne," she smiled. "You certainly seem to have a friend in Heather."

"Heather loves Vikki," Jeremy chuckled. "Maybe more than me."

"No, she doesn't," Vikki said a bit too quickly, tossing

Jeremy a look. "She loves her daddy more than anyone, and you know it."

Jeremy and Vikki visited with his parents for a few more minutes, then headed for the door. As Jeremy said goodbye, his father caught his eye, nodded toward Vikki, and gave a thumbs up. His son stared at him in disbelief.

Jeremy pulled into the tree-lined driveway of the old brick farmhouse and looked over his shoulder. Vikki, catching his glance, looked back too. "She's asleep. Why don't you put her in my guest room? The bed's all made up and you won't have to carry her up the stairs and risk waking her. Anyway, remember you asked me to get her ready and bring her to church tomorrow because of the prayer breakfast."

The church leaders met for an early breakfast on the second Sunday of each month for a time of prayer and fellowship before the service started. Brandon had offered to pick up Jeremy early Sunday morning.

"That's a good idea," Jeremy agreed. "I just don't want her to wake up afraid."

"You can come down early and be there when she wakes up."

"Okay, that sounds good."

Jeremy hoisted Heather out of her car seat and carried her into the house. Vikki led the way to the guest room. He laid her in the bed and then trekked upstairs to get the bedrail from Heather's bed while Vikki went to the kitchen to pour glasses of tea for them.

Jeremy returned with the bedrail, knelt beside Heather, stroked her cheek, and prayed. It was a ritual he had performed each night since Heather had been an infant. Many nights on this journey of fatherhood found Jeremy on his knees raising the despondent prayers of a desperate man, a man who needed help to get through each day and who knew none of the skills required to raise a child. He kissed her cheek. "Goodnight, Angel."

Jeremy found Vikki in the kitchen with eyes frozen on her phone. At the sound of his footsteps, she spun around and stammered, "I'll get us some tea." The color drained from her face, and her eyes were pools of dread.

Jeremy hesitated, wanting to go to her, but a hunch held him in check. He pretended not to notice her unease. He sat down at the table, not taking his eyes off of her, and waited.

Vikki carried the glasses to the table and set one down in front of Jeremy. She sat opposite him and struggled to smile. "I had fun tonight."

An edgy silence saturated the room until Jeremy voiced his concern. "Vikki, I wish you would tell me what's been troubling you today. You've seemed preoccupied and distant since you came home from school. I'm worried about you." He stood and walked to the living room, lowered himself to the couch, and motioned for her to come and join him.

She crossed her arms and rested her head on the table. "I'm fine, I just had a really bad day." She wore a look of complete exhaustion. Jeremy noticed the momentary shift of her eyes to the phone.

"Please come sit by me," Jeremy pleaded, patting the cushion. Vikki sat at the table for a moment more and then plodded over to the couch. "I'm sorry," she said, a sob catching in her throat, "I just can't talk about it." She squeezed her hands together and bowed her head.

"Is it something about Lisa? Did Lee hurt her again?"

Vikki's face crumpled, and she buried her face in her hands, answering his question as clearly as if she had spoken.

"What happened?" his features hardened, "Did he hurt Lisa again or scare you in some way?"

She lifted her head, her eyes a dark green. "No," her voice was too loud, "I just feel helpless, that's all."

Her eyes betrayed her lie. Something had happened, and she was scared. Was it Lisa? Had Lee been at the school again? Anger flared within Jeremy, but he forced himself to remain calm.

He touched her face with his finger and brushed away a tear that trickled down her cheek. "It's okay, Vikki. It's okay." He drew her closer, and she rested her head on his shoulder. He held her without speaking for several minutes, lifting a silent prayer for wisdom. Presently, Vikki straightened herself and rubbed her forehead. "I have a horrible headache."

"Why don't you go get ready for bed and I'll bring you something for your head? Do you have any Tylenol?"

"It's in the bathroom cabinet over the sink," she said as she slowly walked down the hall.

Jeremy stared at the phone. He had to know. He clicked the voicemail button, praying Vikki wouldn't come back into the room.

A few minutes later, Jeremy walked the hallway to Vikki's room and peeked in her door. She had changed into knit pajama bottoms and a t-shirt and was sitting on the side of the bed with her elbows on her knees and her head resting on her fists. "Here, hopefully, this will help your head." He handed her the capsule and glass of water. She swallowed it and set the glass on the table beside her bed.

"Thank you," she whispered.

"Let's get you to bed. Here, let me pull back the blanket." He positioned the sheet and blanket around her as if he were tucking in his daughter. On an impulse, he bent down and kissed her cheek. She turned, and her eyes, dark and troubled, connected with his.

"Do you want me to stay for a while?" he murmured. At Vikki's nod, he slipped under the blanket beside her like it was the most natural thing in the world. Vikki nestled against him, and he held her, stroking her hair in the quiet darkness. Memories of embracing Shannon played in the theater of his mind. He switched off the memories and thought of the troubled girl in his arms now. He would stay just until she fell asleep, then he would get up and sleep on her living room couch.

* * *

Several hours later, Vikki woke up with a start when a slight movement prompted her to roll over. To her amazement, Jeremy was still there. They must have fallen asleep when he was holding her. She gazed down at his sleeping form and let herself imagine what it would be like to wake up next to him each morning. *Don't go there;* she scolded herself and slipped out of bed. Remembering it was Sunday morning, she rummaged in her closet for something to wear to church. She chose black leggings and a light blue dress and carried them into the bathroom.

It was still early, so she decided to make a cup of coffee and relax a few minutes before taking her shower and dressing. Hopefully, by then, Jeremy would wake up. She didn't savor the idea of waking him; it would seem too personal somehow.

As she sat at the table with her head propped in the palms of her hands at the table, she again considered Lee's phone message from the night before. She sipped her coffee and debated whether to meet him as the message had instructed or simply ignore it. But even while she contemplated, she knew that she would meet him as he had demanded.

Deep in thought, Vikki jumped at the sound of the doorbell. She glanced at the clock, it read 6:30. "Who could be here so early?" she murmured to herself. She padded to the door and opened it to find Pastor Brandon wearing an awkward smile. "Well, hello, Pastor," she said, waiting for him to make known his intentions.

"Hello, Miss Thompson, I'm looking for Jeremy," he said apologetically, "I couldn't get anyone to answer his door, so I thought maybe there was an interior entrance to the apartment."

Flustered, Vikki groped for a response. She had completely forgotten about the prayer meeting. Maybe she could have him wait in the living room while she ran down the hallway to rouse Jeremy and somehow get him up the stairway without being seen by Brandon. "Well, there is a stairway off my kitchen," she stated, opening the door for him to enter, "Why don't you…"

At that moment, Jeremy, still dressed in his jeans and now wrinkled t-shirt, his hair tousled from a night of slumber, ambled barefoot from the hallway into the front room, crossing directly in front of Brandon, who had stepped into the entryway. "Oh," he said, sharing a startled look with Vikki.

Brandon's face showed no emotion except for a slight lift of his eyebrows. "Hello, Jeremy, I guess I knocked on the wrong door before," he alleged with a meaningful look.

Suddenly, Jeremy remembered. "Oh man, the prayer breakfast!" he exclaimed. "I am so sorry, Brandon. It completely slipped my mind." He rubbed his temple. "I'll be ready in just a minute." He stole a quick look toward the stairs and pursed his lips. He glanced at the stairway. "I—uh—I need to go upstairs for a minute," he stammered and paused, "I'll be right down.

Just then, the voice of a child called out from the guest bedroom, "Daddy, I want up." Brandon's eyes widened as Jeremy's eyes closed—the final nail.

"I think I'll wait in the car," Brandon said and walked out the door.

CHAPTER TWENTY-ONE

The early morning sky was just birthing its pageant of yellow and red as Jeremy and Brandon traveled along the country road. Jeremy would have enjoyed God's artistry more if his companion had not been so solemn. The prayer breakfast was at the local Steak and Shake, and it was sure to be bustling this Sunday morning. Claymon enjoyed few restaurant choices, and franchise operations were even scarcer. Steak and Shake, situated off the interstate exchange, did very well.

Jeremy chanced a sideways glance at Brandon, who sat silently as he drove. He supposed his pastor was waiting for some explanation about the morning's events ,but having nothing acceptable to offer; he stared out the front window taking in the promise of a beautiful display in the heavens. Unnerved by Brandon's silence, he shifted in his seat, "I hope we won't be too late. I'm sorry I forgot about the breakfast," he apologized.

"We won't be. I guess you had your mind on other things," Brandon replied without taking his eyes off the road.

Great, so much for conversation. "It's not what you think," Jeremy countered, catching Brandon's meaning.

"I think you spent the night with your girlfriend," came Brandon's candid reply.

"Touché," he smothered his amusement. "But she's not my girlfriend, and what you're thinking isn't true. Nothing happened."

Brandon turned into the restaurant lot and killed the engine. He studied Jeremy for several long, uncomfortable seconds as if he was sizing up a wayward child. "Jeremy, I'm going to take your word on this because I believe you to be an honest man, although," his features softened and the mere trace of a smile tugged the corners of his mouth, "I also believe you're in denial about your feelings for Vikki."

"Thank you, Brandon," Jeremy said. His features lifted in relief.

"Oh, you're not off the hook, Son. Not by a long shot. I want to see you in my office right after the second service this morning. I'd like to hear a little more about your night."

Jeremy bit his lip and blew out a puff of air. Meeting with Brandon after the second service presented a problem since he wanted to be close by when Vikki met with Lee. But Jeremy knew his pastor well enough; he indeed wasn't off the hook. And what was this nonsense about denial?

* * *

Jeremy sat in the front pew before the first service began and prayed he could overcome the morning's distractions and concentrate on his sermon. He had developed the message, *Doing the Right Thing When the Right Thing Costs You,* over several weeks. The theme was that often doing the right thing doesn't cost us much emotionally or physically. Specific moral values are taught and accepted as part of the

Christian lifestyle, and for the most part, the choices are
easily discernible and "cost-effective"—they don't hurt much.
When the correct option appears too difficult or too
unpleasant, "costly," we try to rationalize our poor choices.
We say things like: "God doesn't want His children to be
unhappy," "God will understand why I have to do this," "The
end justifies the means," "I'm sure God wouldn't expect that
of me," or even, "Jesus hung around sinners, too. I will never
fall into their sin."

Though he knew it was a familiar theme, Jeremy planned
to present it with a new angle, one that prompted his
listeners to examine their own choices, even the hard ones,
making sure they made the right choice despite the cost.

Jeremy was a talented speaker. He could capture his audience's attention, bring them to his point of view, challenge
them without seeming "preachy" or condemning, partly
because of his humble nature, always including himself in
any shortcomings, and partly because of his natural
charisma. Today was no exception. Jeremy recognized from
the expressions on his audience's faces that he had made a
connection, though he knew it was by God's grace that he
was even able to get through his message this morning.

New Life Community had its Sunday school hour
between services. Jeremy stood in the lobby, mingling as
expected while anxiously waiting for Vikki and Heather to
arrive for Sunday school. He didn't like the tone of the voicemail he had eavesdropped on as it played again in his mind.
"Meet me in the library after the second service. I have something to show you. Don't mess with me. Be there or you
won't be the only one to pay." He recognized Lee's voice and
had witnessed the fear it had triggered in Vikki.

Vikki held Heather's hand as they approached the church
door to attend Sunday school. Jeremy rushed over and
opened it for them. "Hi," he said as he guided them over to a

corner. "Well, I made it to the restaurant in one piece and," he managed a slight grin, "I convinced Brandon that we weren't living in sin. Unfortunately, he still wants to see me right after church."

Vikki's eyes fell, "I'm sorry, Jeremy. I was a mess last night. I shouldn't have put you in such a position."

"You were upset. I couldn't leave you," Jeremy whispered, lifting her chin. "I want to tell you something; I didn't plan on falling asleep with you. I woke up in the middle of the night, and I should have got up immediately. But I didn't. I just held you closer and went back to sleep. I didn't want to leave." He looked away for a moment. "There's something else," he added. "I listened to the message on your phone last night while you were getting ready for bed."

"Oh," she replied, her lips parting a little. "You know about me meeting Lee, then."

"Yes. I'm sorry that I invaded your privacy, but you seemed so upset, and I knew it had to do with the message you received."

"It's okay," she squeezed his hand. "I have to meet him, you know."

"I figured that, and I want to follow you, but Brandon is serious about meeting with me."

"I don't think you should follow me anyway. Lee might see you. He said he had something to show me. I don't think he will hurt me or anything," she said, forcing a brave tone. But her fear was evident as she lifted her gaze.

Jeremy wrapped his arms around her and pulled her close, unaware that Brandon stood not ten feet away. "Father, protect and lead Vikki in this meeting with Lee. Let no harm come to her," he prayed. He held her at arm's length. "We'd better get to class before Brandon comes looking for me. Or, maybe we should consider another class," he teased, "one without Brandon or Lee in it."

The pair walked Heather to her classroom and then slipped into their Sunday school class, drawing interest from several people, including a meaningful half-smile from Alice Winters, a knowing look from Brandon, who had just seated himself, and a smirk from Lee. Jeremy groaned inwardly. *Welcome to class.*

Lisa was not seated next to Lee, and Vikki figured she had stayed home so she wouldn't draw questions about her broken arm. She hoped Lee hadn't hurt her anymore. Vikki kept her eyes focused on her reading material and hugged her arms close to her body, sensing Lee's bold scrutiny. The teacher's words drifted in the air and fell meaningless into her ears.

* * *

Jeremy prayed silently during the praise and worship portion of the second service, knowing that it would be difficult to keep his focus with both Lee and Vikki in attendance. He managed to get through his message by making sure he did not look at either one of them, and once again, he felt a connection with the people.

After the service, Jeremy was so distracted he barely noticed the numerous compliments people offered as he greeted them automatically, saying the appropriate words by rote. He kept an eye out for Vikki or Lee but saw neither one leave the sanctuary. As soon as he could gracefully escape the crowd, he dashed down the hall toward the library, nearly careening into Brandon.

Brandon held up his hands. "Hold on, where are you going in such a hurry? Remember, I want to talk to you."

Jeremy kept his head turned toward the direction of his destination, "Right, I remember. I need to pick up Heather first and, uh—talk to Vikki for a minute." He rushed on down the hall, "I'll be right there," he tossed behind him, leaving Brandon muttering to himself and shaking his head.

Jeremy raced to the library door, wondering if Vikki was already with Lee. He peeked around the door and saw two people in the far corner behind the last bookshelf. Jeremy inched along the wall a few feet and situated himself at the end of the first row of shelving closest to the door. The library was on the small side, so he dared not get any nearer. He could barely make out Lee's voice. "I hope you had fun at your concert last night. Oh, and, I have some pictures." He heard Vikki's soft gasp but could not make out what she was saying.

"That's right. I had a detective friend tail you and take pictures just to show you I meant business when I told you to keep your mouth shut," he laughed with spite. "But lucky me, Jeremy was there with you, and I got these as a bonus. I believe they show an interesting side of our preacher."

Jeremy dropped to his knees as Lee looked in his direction. He crawled to the door and met curious gazes when he entered the hallway on his knees. He rose to his feet and then half-ran the straight shot to the preschool room, careening into an older lady with his shoulder and knocking her Bible out of her hand.

"Excuse me, I am so sorry." He snatched up the Bible and thrust it out to the teetering woman. "I hope I didn't hurt you."

"Oh, it's okay. Your sermon wasn't too bad," the dazed lady uttered.

He had to smile at her reply. If his sermon was actually good, he'd have a free pass for assault and battery in the hallways of the church. "Thanks," he threw over his shoulder as he continued his rush to Heather's class.

After apologizing for his tardiness, he took Heather by the hand and half dragged her down the hallway. Vikki walked out the library door ahead of him, looking shaken but unharmed. She glanced his way but continued her stride forward, with Lee lagging behind her. Jeremy met up with Vikki in the foyer, where she took Heather's hand. "I'll take her home. Good luck." She walked out the door without further comment.

Jeremy waited until he saw Vikki back out of her parking space, then zipped toward Brandon's office, gathered his resolve, and knocked on the half-open door.

"Come in."

"Sorry it took me a few minutes."

Brandon nodded. "Have a seat." He regarded Jeremy for a moment as if unsure of how to proceed. Then his expression lightened. "Before we discuss your activities from last night, I want you to know that your message was exceptional this morning. I was impressed, and so were a lot of other people. You have a gift, Jeremy."

"Thanks." Jeremy beamed at the compliment. "I really worked hard on the sermon, but I only got through it this morning by the grace of God," he said, with heartfelt meaning.

Brandon took a deep breath and exhaled. "Jeremy, I don't relish prying into people's personal lives. It is one of the aspects of my job I dislike the most. Nevertheless, it is necessary at times," he sighed and frowned a little. "Unfortunately, this is one of those times since you are a church leader."

Jeremy locked eyes with his pastor. "I have nothing to hide, Brandon."

"Good." The senior minister drew out the word and tapped his desk with a pencil. "Tell me then, how did you end up spending the night with Vikki?"

"I'm not sure where to begin. It really isn't that interesting."

"Oh, I like boring stories," Brandon rested his chin on his

fingers, elbows on the table. "In this case, the more boring your story, the better for you. Wouldn't you agree?"

Jeremy couldn't stifle a slight smile. "Yeah, I guess so." He explained about getting home late from the concert and how Vikki had suggested letting Heather sleep in her guest room. He went on to tell how Vikki became very upset about an incident at school. At this point, he hesitated, realizing the following words were crucial.

Brandon, whose eyes had remained fixed on Jeremy, prompted him. "I'm listening, please continue."

Jeremy met his eyes briefly and then rested his gaze on Brandon's desk. He would lay his cards on the table and watch the hand play out. "Like I said, Vikki was very emotional. She wouldn't tell me what had happened at school, but I know it had to do with Lee abusing his wife."

Brandon's eyes flashed at that information, but he didn't interrupt Jeremy.

"She complained of a terrible headache and got ready for bed. I found some Tylenol and took it to her." He sighed and let out a slow sigh, "I didn't want to leave because I was afraid for her well-being. I only planned to stay until she fell asleep, but... I fell asleep, too," he finished under his breath, fully aware of the conclusion Brandon would draw.

Brandon stared at his desk as if weighing his next words. He lifted his eyes to meet Jeremy's. "Did you sleep in her bed?"

Jeremy rubbed his finger slowly across his lip, "Yes." He held his minister's eyes for several seconds. "Nothing happened, Brandon. The jeans and t-shirt I had on this morning are what I wore all night. I never so much as kissed her. I only held her because she needed me to. There's nothing else to tell." He rubbed his temples, dreading the doubt and disapproval he was sure Brandon would voice.

Brandon folded his hands on the table and tilted his head

slightly. "It's a unique story, I'll give you that." He pursed his lips and continued. "I believe you, Jeremy, though your judgment was debatable at best. It's understandable why you wouldn't want to leave her, but to place yourself in that circumstance was irresponsible, especially for a man in your position. It's like playing with fire. You are not above falling to temptation. I'm sure you realize the firestorm this kind of information would cause if certain people got a hold of it."

"Yes, I do," Jeremy breathed, "but there was no temptation involved."

Brandon leaned back in his chair, resting his chin on his fingertips, his expression growing thoughtful. "You say that Vikki is just a friend, yet your actions and words betray you."

"She is just a friend," Jeremy retorted.

"I'm sorry, Jeremy, I've seen how you are with her. I saw you embracing her this morning. I just listened to you talk about her, watched the emotions play out on your face, and I find it difficult to believe that your feelings are purely platonic."

"I guess that's your choice," Jeremy scoffed.

Brandon ignored his insolence and pressed the point. "Can you look me in the eye and honestly tell me you don't have feelings beyond friendship for Vikki?"

Jeremy's head swam as he sat in silence, his eyes closed and his hands gripping the arms of the chair for so long that Brandon shifted in his seat uncomfortably. "No... I—I can't," Jeremy finally managed. His face paled as he dropped his head in his hands, unable to accept the truth he voiced.

"Then, why are you fighting it so hard?"

Jeremy rebuked him with fiery eyes. "You know why. I loved someone once," he snapped, struggling for control, shocked at the intense anger pulsing through his body, "and God took her from me. I won't, I can't ever love anyone again." He sat rigidly with his fists closed in a tight ball.

Brandon knew of Shannon's death, but none of the details, other than the fact her baby was born after her death. He pressed further, his voice calm, "Are you going to refuse to fall in love again to punish God... or yourself?"

Stunned by the question, Jeremy groped for words. "All I know is I loved Shannon, and I failed her." He bit out his words as he struggled to cling to his last thread of control. "God snatched her out of my life."

"You can't blame yourself for her death."

Jeremy shot him a scathing look and leaned toward him. "Don't you say that. You don't understand," his eyes narrowed, and he pressed his fingers on his forehead. "Have you ever watched someone you loved be assaulted and murdered?" Brandon flinched at the fury in Jeremy's voice.

Jeremy jerked his chair back and shot to his feet. Unleashed rage pounded through his body. He stormed across the room and slammed his fist into the windowpane and then the wall. He gripped the edge of the windowsill, grappling for some shred of rational thought, awed and terri-fied of emotions so long suppressed now spewing from his heart and soul. The control he had fought so hard to hold on to since Shannon's death was crumbling, and it terrified him. His body trembled as he stood at the window, helpless against the relentless onslaught of excruciating memories.

Visibly shaken by Jeremy's intense emotion, Brandon took tentative steps toward the agonized young preacher and waited for his wrath to dissipate. Jeremy spun around to face him, trembling with guilt-fueled passion. "I heard her beg for mercy," he uttered with undisguised anguish. "I heard her scream out my name. They beat me and held me down as I helplessly watched. I... couldn't... save her." His face twisted as he inhaled ragged breaths, "I failed her. And so did God," he said in a choked whisper. His body slid down the wall to the floor.

Brandon's eyes were moist as he realized the horror Jeremy had witnessed. "And you can't forgive yourself... or God," he asserted.

"God doesn't need my forgiveness," Jeremy said with clipped words.

"No, he doesn't need it, but you need to offer it. You have to forgive God and then yourself. But before you can move on you need to face your anger, embrace it, understand it, and then let it go."

Let go of the anger, Jeremy. It will tear you apart. Shannon's voice drifted through his soul as it did the first night he knelt at her gravesite. *Let go of the anger, Jeremy.* "I don't know how," Jeremy's voice cracked, and his head drooped.

"Let me pray with you," Brandon invited, laying his hand on Jeremy's shoulder.

"Don't you think I've tried that... over and over?"

"But maybe you couldn't be ready until you faced your anger and feelings of guilt." Brandon kneeled on the floor beside Jeremy. "Are you ready now? May I help you talk to God?"

Jeremy sat with his head on his knees and cried out the torment he'd kept locked in his spirit. After several minutes he looked at Brandon seated cross-legged on the floor beside him. "I don't know how to get over this. I thought I was okay, but clearly—*clearly* I'm not. I thought I could ignore the pain, and it would somehow go away. I thought I would get over it by now."

"I'm not sure getting over it is the goal. I think you have to acknowledge your anger and resentment."

Jeremy nodded and looked at Brandon with doubtful eyes, "But what right do I have to be angry with God? I have fought this for so long. I'm so tired of the struggle."

"God only wants our honesty. He already knows our

emotions, good and bad. You can deny them before me and others, but not God. He understands what is in your heart."

Jeremy bowed, broken before God. "I know. I've tried so hard not to feel anything because it hurts too much and the emotions scare me. Shannon called my name, and I couldn't help her. That haunts me when my mind goes to dark places."

Brandon put his hand on Jeremy's shoulder. "And God knows all of it. He wants you to surrender that guilt and anger. You have no fault in what happened to Shannon. Do you believe she is in heaven?" Jeremy nodded. Brandon touched Jeremy's hand. "Shannon loved you, and I don't believe she would want you to have this guilt. God wants to release you from your guilt. He wants to give you hope and a purpose."

Jeremy stared at Brandon. There was that verse again. Maybe it was time to claim it. His tears flowed without shame as he acknowledged his resentment toward God and his guilt over not being able to save Shannon. Anger that had smoldered since Shannon's death flowed from his innermost being like a river carrying with it the burden of doubt and bitterness that had sealed his heart. Unable to form the words, his heart cried out to God as he let the Holy Spirit intercede for him.

Brandon laid his hands on Jeremy and petitioned God on his behalf. "Our Father in heaven, I lift up your broken child. Fill his heart and soul with your peace. Let your grace flow over the fear and anger plaguing his heart. Give him the strength to face and then reject his guilt. Restore his joy and bless his gift of spreading your word. I pray for all these requests in Jesus' name. Amen."

Several minutes later, the two men stood and walked back to Brandon's desk.

"Thank you, Brandon," Jeremy said, his voice still unsteady. "I didn't realize the rage I had in my soul." He gave his head a sad shake. "I feel empty. But I know I can be honest in my prayers now, and the Lord will fill the spaces with His grace."

Brandon nodded. "You needed to release your anger before you could be liberated from your chains." He met Jeremy's eyes. "You're free now, and God can fill the emptiness. If you let Him guide you, you will become even more effective as a preacher. We can talk more later about how to grow your faith through all of this."

"I'd appreciate that." Jeremy glanced at the clock and stood up, "I need to go now. Vikki will wonder what has happened to me. Thanks again. You've helped me so much."

Brandon smiled, "You already knew the answer. I just provided the push. Goodbye, Jeremy," he tilted his head, "and behave yourself."

"Always," Jeremy managed a shaky grin and winked.

CHAPTER TWENTY-TWO

Jordan stole a look at Jessie from behind the wheel. She had shared the threatening call from Lee with him on the way to church this morning. "It concerns me, Jessie, that Lee would call and threaten you like that. He must really be a nutcase."

"He's afraid his wife will remember my name and put two and two together. To be honest, he scared me to death when he called, but now that I think about it, I'm sure he was trying to do just that. I also think he had been drinking."

"You're probably right, but if he calls again you need to record the call and notify the police. Maybe you can stay somewhere else for a while."

"Like where?"

"Well, how about Vikki? I'm sure she'd let you stay a few nights until you're sure he's not going to bother you. She wouldn't have to know anything other than you're getting threatening phone calls from some nutjob."

Jessie shrugged and looked out the passenger window as Jordan drove down a country road. Though many trees had already shed their leaves, the orange, red, and yellow display was still vibrant along this route. "I don't know, Jordan. I'll think about it." She patted his knee. "Thank you for going with me to my parent's church."

"No problem. It was good." He gave up, for now, on the subject of Jessie staying with someone. "I see where Jeremy gets his talent for speaking," he said, changing the subject. "Your father's message really held my attention."

"Yes, they are both great speakers, Jeremy's style is a little different, though."

"Yeah, I agree, he puts a little more personality in his presentation, where your father is more old school, I guess. But I enjoyed his sermon." He squeezed her hand. "And we all got to know one another over dinner. Do you think I passed the test?"

"They loved you. I could tell, especially my mother. You really turned on the charm." She flashed him a smile.

"Hey, I'm just naturally charming—especially to beautiful ladies," he joked.

Jordan slowed as they neared her apartment and pulled into a parking spot. He turned to face Jessie. "I've been wondering something about your brother. Are you free to tell me more about his wife's death? I know that she died in childbirth, and, I don't know, he always seems troubled whenever we approach that subject. I kinda thought there was more to the story."

Sadness shadowed Jessie's amber eyes. "She was murdered, Jordan."

"Murdered? Oh, I'm sorry. You don't have to tell me about it."

"No, it's okay. I don't think Jeremy would mind."

Sadness and shock crossed Jordan's face as Jessie shared all she knew about Shannon's death. She finished with a sigh, "I really didn't know if he was going to make it for a while, but he was determined to raise

Heather. I think he has done a remarkable job with that."

"Man, what a burden to carry around. He is a strong person, that's for sure."

"I hope he finds true happiness again one day." They sat in silence for a few minutes, and then Jessie drew in her breath. "Well, I guess we should get out of the car."

Jordan took her hand, and they made their way to Jessie's apartment door. "Do you want to come in for a while?"

"I don't know if I should, Jessie. I'm not sure I can trust myself alone with you," he half-joked.

"Well," she held her head at an angle, "we could go to the mall and hang out for a while." She opened the door and stepped in. "Come in for a minute, anyway."

"Sure, we can hang out at the mall." Jordan walked in and stood in the small entryway.

"Sit down on the couch and I'll be right back. I am going to change."

"Into something more comfortable?" Jordan quipped.

"Yes, jeans and a sweater," she shot back.

"Oh well."

After a few minutes, Jessie appeared in the living room wearing the promised blue jeans and a yellow sweater. Jordan allowed his gaze to drift over her. He reached for her hand, pulled her down on the couch beside him, and gave her a lingering kiss. "I love you, Jessie."

Jessie snuggled against his shoulder and traced his cheek with her finger. "I love you, too." She kissed him and wrapped her arms around his neck.

"Hey," he said softly, finding her far too alluring, "Let's go to the mall like you said."

She sat up, her eyes shining. "Okay, just to hang out?"

"Oh, I don't know, I might have something I want you to look at," He smiled like a mischievous boy.

She tilted her head. "What?"

"Diamonds," he said as innocently as he could.

Jessie sat up straight. "Jordan Raycom, what are you talking about?"

He took her hands and brought them to his lips. "I love you. I want you with me forever. You know, marry me."

Jessie's jaw dropped. "Are you serious?"

"I've never been more serious. I've waited a long time for a girl like you." He pulled her to him and brushed her cheek with his lips. "I love you and I want to be with you as your husband," he said, his eyes searching hers for approval.

Jessie was aware of his face, his appealing smile, and his eyes bright with love. She eyed him for a long moment. "But, Jordan, you know I haven't always lived like a Christian."

"Hey," he whispered and turned her face toward him. "We've been all through that, remember? It doesn't matter to me. You believe Jesus died for your sins, right."

"Yes, but…"

"Then your mistakes are in the past. Leave them there. Accept God's forgiveness and don't let Satan accuse you any longer."

"But I can't accept everything the church I grew up in stands for."

He angled his head and lifted the corners of his mouth. "I didn't ask about your views on the church. I asked about your salvation. And besides," he gave a sly smile, "our different views might make for stimulating conversation."

She felt the gentle pressure of his finger as he wiped a tear sliding down her cheek. He lifted her face and slowly kissed away her doubts. When the kiss broke, she smiled up at him.

"Are you serious? I mean about getting married."

"Sure. I love you."

"Well, we haven't known each other very long. What time frame were you thinking about?"

He longed to kiss her again. "Right now," he teased, attempting to lighten the mood. "Or if you need a little more time, how about next Saturday?"

"I'm serious, Jordan."

"So am I. I know we haven't known each other very long, but I am positive about this. You are an answer to prayer. It feels right." He put his arm around her and drew her close again. "Tell me, just how long would it take to plan the wedding of your dreams?"

Jessie sat upright and cast a broad smile, "Oh Jordan, some people take a whole year to plan an elegant wedding!" she exclaimed.

Jordan's eyes were saucers. "A whole year?"

She giggled in delight and poked him in the side. "Oh, you know I wouldn't want a big fancy wedding." She climbed on his lap with her knees on either side of him, draping her arms around his neck. Her eyes dazzled him with mischief. "But, honestly, I would need four or five months at least. Besides," she tousled his hair, "we need time to get to know each other as an engaged couple."

Right now, with his heart beating wildly against his chest, five months seemed a lifetime. "Okay," he breathed, "But let's go to the mall now, Love."

They strolled to the car in the brisk air, Jordan's head reeling with the memory of her fingers stroking his face and running through his hair.

* * *

Jeremy and Vikki glided on the porch swing, watching Heather play in her Little Tykes car. The air was crisp, but the sun made it comfortable. Jeremy told Vikki the details of his visit with Brandon, leaving out the part about his true feelings for her. She sat quietly, absorbing every detail, her facial features running the gamut from horror to sorrow to quiet joy as he brought the story to an end. "The most important thing is I am finally dealing with my anger and resentment, and I am learning to forgive myself for not being able to save Shannon. I also had to forgive God, and ask for His forgiveness. It seems so wrong, though, to be angry with the creator of the universe."

"But if you are angry, God knows that anyway."

He shook his head and smiled a little bit. "That's what Brandon said."

After swinging in silence for a few minutes, Jeremy voiced the question he had been waiting to ask. "Do you want to tell me about your meeting with Lee this morning?"

"There's nothing much to tell. He just warned me not to tell anyone he beats up his wife," she uttered with frustration.

Jeremy stopped the swing and pivoted so he could look at her face. "I followed you and hid in the church library, Vikki. What pictures did Lee have?"

"Oh," she muttered, "He actually hired someone to follow me. Do you believe that? I don't understand why, other than to intimidate me. Anyway, he took pictures of us at the concert and had them printed." She shuddered. "It really creeps me out. He knows where I live and has resorted to having someone follow me."

"Yeah, it bothers me, too. It would be easy enough to find out where you live, I guess. But to have you followed would suggest that Lee has a lot of fear about what you know and might tell. He is sending a message to shut you up. Did he show you the pictures? I heard him say he had questionable photos of me."

"He just flashed them at me, and it was dark in the library.

I couldn't see much. I can't imagine what would be so interesting about them."

Jeremy tilted his head. "I don't know. We were acting a little crazy, I guess. He probably thought I was drinking, and he knows Brandon's position on that," he paused for a second, "or any questionable behavior that involves a leader in the church. Lee made it pretty clear that I wasn't his first choice for an associate pastor, but I didn't think he was out to get me fired or anything. It all seems so strange."

"Well," she said and sat up straighter, "I decided today that I can't sit idly by anymore knowing what I know. I think I should tell Brandon, don't you?"

Jeremy considered the ramifications that action might bring. Wasn't it the right thing to do, though? Didn't he preach only this morning about doing the right thing even if it was costly? "Yes, I think you probably have no choice at this point. Have you thought about getting the police involved?"

"Yes, but I assumed they wouldn't be able to do anything unless Lisa reported it."

"They might send out child protective services if the abuse has occurred when her little girl was present," Jeremy stated. He gave her a long look. "Will you tell me what happened Saturday morning that upset you so much?"

She turned away from his scrutiny but not before he saw fear color her face. He turned her shoulders so that she faced him. "Did Lee touch you?" he demanded.

"No," her voice wavered.

"Don't lie to me, Vikki." He tightened his grip on her, frustration flitting across his features.

She twisted out of his hold, her eyes flashing with anger. "I'm not your child," she said through clenched teeth. "He pinned me against the wall and threatened me, but he didn't hurt me, okay?" Her hands trembled at the memory.

Jeremy's fists clenched in anger as the vision of Lee pinning Vikki against the wall played out in his mind. He took hold of her hands and drew her close. "I know you're not a child," he said and took a deep breath to calm himself. "I just can't tolerate the thought of him threatening you or hurting you in any way."

She brought her hand to her mouth. "Her arm was broken, Jeremy. She said she fell down the stairs. No way do I believe that. I have to tell someone."

"Is that why you were so upset, Saturday?"

"Yes, he threatened to hurt Lisa more if I told anyone." She twisted her necklace.

"Well, I'll go with you to see Brandon if you want to wait until my shift at the fire station ends Tuesday. This is Jordan's overnight stretch, so I am scheduled with him. I've already arranged for Heather to stay the night with my parents. I can make the appointment after four on Tuesday afternoon."

"Thanks, I would like that. Do you think Brandon will believe me?"

Jeremy cupped his hands around her face, unable to tear his eyes from her fear-filled ones. "We'll have to persuade him somehow."

"Okay," Vikki whispered. "I have a lot of papers to grade, so I guess I'd better get busy."

Jeremy squeezed her hands. "That's fine, I have to take Heather to my parents' house in a bit anyway. I'll call and set up an appointment with Brandon for Tuesday. Everything will be all right."

Jeremy corralled Heather, and the three of them walked into the house. He hesitated at the stairway door that led to his apartment and drew Vikki into a soft hug. He dipped his head without speaking, and his lips almost touched hers before they kissed her cheek. "Goodbye, Vikki. I'll see you Tuesday afternoon."

Jeremy packed Heather's suitcase and drove her to his mom and dad's house, then came home to rest for a few hours before leaving for work.

As he climbed the steps to his apartment, he wondered why he kept struggling against his feelings for Vikki. He would never win this battle, no matter how fiercely he fought, because he'd already lost the war.

He went into the living room and collapsed on his sofa bed, letting the events of the emotionally charged day play through his mind, draining his last reserve of resistance. His eyes closed in weariness.

* * *

The demon dragon ferociously pursued its victim. Even as Jeremy clawed at the ground, his fingers raw and bleeding, he felt the dragon's strength swell, dragging him into the pit. His fingers clung to the edge, raking the dirt side as he slid ever downward. Exhausted from the struggle, he felt himself slipping as his body surrendered to the darkness. It was over. He could fight no longer. As he spiraled down into the pit, he felt a force of some sort drawing him from above, unwilling to give him up to the dragon's terrible realm. Thus began a great tug of war in which he was the pawn. The dragon pulled him ever lower into dark shadows, but the power from above refused to release him to the blackness. A voice implored him, "Let go of the demon. Let go."

"I can't let go. The dragon's gripping me," he faltered, "and hauling me down to the bottom of the pit."

"No, it's you. You alone have the power to unshackle yourself. You are clutching onto the dragon. Let go. You are the one who must release," said the voice, with more urgency now.

In that moment of desperation, his eyes proclaimed the truth. The dragon had no grip on him. No, it was he who grasped the dragon's wing. The demon dragon plummeted toward the depths of the pit with willing prey.

"I'm afraid," he shrieked, "I can't let go."

"You must. It is the only way out."

Frantic, he tried to release the dragon's wing, but his hands refused to unwrap their panicked hold. "I can't. I'll fall!" he cried.

A familiar voice drifted into his consciousness and begged him, "Let go of your anger and guilt, Jeremy. It is killing your soul. Let go of the demon within you that stokes up your anguish. Let go. You won't fall."

He tilted his head upward to the dazzling golden radiance and drew from its power. He willed his fingers on his right hand to break their grip on the dragon's wing, but the fingers on his left hand responded by increasing their hold, leaving him dangling over the pit with one arm. Hungry flames leaped out and nipped his feet. He felt his skin blister from the heat. "I'll fall into the pit," he screamed.

"No, you won't fall!" the voice shouted above the roar of the ever-nearing fire. "You have to let go, or you will plummet into the pit along with the demon."

Panic threatened to overpower him as Jeremy pried two more fingers off the dragon's wing with his free hand, and his feet burned as they dangled over the eager flames waiting to devour him. His eyes groped for the glorious light, now growing dim in the fiery smoke, for it was his only source of hope and power. He cried out in torment and summoned his last ounce of strength. He tore his remaining fingers from the dragon's wing.

Blinding light engulfed him, and he let out a scream as he

began to freefall into the terrible glowing pit. At that moment, the glorious force thrust him upwards and out of the dragon's reach. Infuriated, it let out a mind-numbing screech of rage, surrendered its victim, and plummeted into the depths of Hell.

Jeremy bolted upright. His eyes roamed the dimly lit room in confusion, and he wiped the sweat dripping from his brow. Where was he? Slowly, the fogginess lifted. He'd been dreaming, but it was more than a dream. It was as if great chains had been torn from him—chains of bondage. Something, or someone, had snatched him from the dragon's claws, the dragon that had haunted him since Shannon's death. No, that wasn't true. He squeezed his eyes and waited for clarity. No outside force released him. He had freed himself with the help of the radiant light from above. Jeremy tapped his phone to check the time. It felt much later than nine.

He knelt by his bed, praying without words. The final residues of dread lifted from his soul. After his prayer, he felt compelled to see Vikki. Dancing down the steps with newfound freedom, he felt his heart pound with joy for the first time since Shannon's death.

Jeremy tapped on the door, hoping that Vikki was still awake. Then, not waiting for her to answer, he opened it. She stood at the sink in a short blue satin gown with spaghetti straps, holding a glass in her hand and gazing with surprise at her renter.

"Oh, hi." She brought her free hand to her chest. "Come in. Let me get my robe."

Jeremy crossed the room allowing his eyes to linger on her, and gave her a flirty smile, "I kinda like the gown." He lifted her chin, tucked her hair behind her ear, and traced her jaw with his fingers. His lips touched hers tentatively, and longing rose within his spirit. The uncertainty on her face tugged at his heart. Jeremy touched her lips again with a slow, sweet kiss. Vikki's wide, emerald eyes delved into the hidden places of his heart, dissolving any remnants of the walls he had erected.

"I love you, Vikki. I had to come tell you."

"But, I thought…" she whispered.

"It's okay. I'm free from the guilt, Vikki. I let it go. I'll always have a place in my heart for Shannon, but," he took her hands in his, "I believe I can feel love again." Their lips met in a lingering kiss. "I love you."

Vikki wrapped her arms around his neck and smiled up at him, "I love you, too."

He held her in his arms, and they gently swayed back and forth. "I've loved you a long time, Vikki. I just couldn't accept it."

Vikki's green eyes grew troubled, and she stepped back a few paces. "Jeremy, we need to talk about something."

Her tone was so serious, he knew she had something important to say. "Sure, but could we talk upstairs? I left my phone up there, and I need to call and check on Heather before I leave for work. And, oh, you might want to get your robe after all," he said, glancing at her gown with a little bit of a grin.

* * *

Vikki looked uncomfortable as she sat next to Jeremy on his sofa, sipping the water he had poured for her.

"You wanted to talk about something?" Jeremy prompted.

"Yes, I need to tell you something about my past before we go any further in our relationship."

His eyes told her he doubted anything in her past would jeopardize their relationship. He reached for her hand. "Tell me, Vikki. Whatever it is, we will work through it."

She twisted a strand of her hair around her finger and fixed her gaze on her lap. "I've been married before." She stole a glance at him to gauge his response, but she couldn't read his expression. "I'm divorced."

"Do you want to tell me about it?" He took the glass from her other hand and placed it on the small table beside the couch. He turned sideways and waited for her to continue.

Her voice trembled as she began her story. "I came home early from dinner with my sister one night and caught Tom, my husband, with another woman." She took a shaky breath. "I packed a bag and left that night. We were divorced within two months."

Jeremy raised her head so he could see her eyes and held her hands in his. "I'm so sorry that you were hurt like that. That guy must have been crazy to cheat on you, but it doesn't change how I feel about you in any way."

Vikki hesitated as if uncertain how to continue. She pulled her hands away. "I know some churches have strict rules about their ministers and who they—well... you know." Her cheeks grow rosy.

The pink blush made her look so adorable he wanted to take her in his arms, but he stifled the urge. "Vikki, the Bible permits divorce in certain cases, adultery being one of them," he explained. "I don't think there will be any problem. Anyway, no one in the church needs to know you were married before." A smile tugged at the corners of his mouth, "Except maybe Brandon during our counseling sessions."

Vikki tilted her head and gave him a curious look. "What do you mean?"

"Well," he fiddled with the belt on her robe, "Brandon always does prenuptial counseling." He watched her face turn a deeper pink as he feigned an innocent confusion. "I mean— you were asking me to marry you, weren't you?"

"You are so rotten," Vikki laughed at his jest. She picked up a sofa pillow and hit him in the face.

He grabbed it and whacked her playfully on the head. "Me? What did I do?" he asked.

She tried to grab the pillow again, but he tossed it behind him and took hold of her shoulders. "Seriously, Vikki, it doesn't matter to me. I've been married before too, you know." His voice wavered, "I would be honored to have you for my wife someday."

She lowered her head. "I swore I would never trust a man again."

"He was a fool."

"Apparently, I wasn't good enough for him."

"No, he didn't deserve you. I will make sure you have no reason to doubt me."

The evening on the balcony wafted into Jeremy's mind. He rubbed her thumb lightly as he held her hand. "That's the reason you reacted so strongly the first time I kissed you, isn't it? I misled you into thinking I wasn't interested in you because I had someone else." He sighed and smiled at her. "Vikki, you're lovely. I've been attracted to you since the day I came to look at the apartment and you got all flustered when you assumed I was married. I spent a whole lot of energy fighting it, though."

Vikki's eyes dimmed. "I do love you, Jeremy. But if we do decide to get married, I am not sure I'm cut out to be a preacher's wife."

"Why?"

Vikki frowned. "I'm not as friendly as you and don't find it easy to walk up to people and introduce myself, and I'm not sure I would fit the role of entertaining very well."

"Vikki, just be yourself. I wouldn't put any pressure on you to be the perfect preacher's wife. I love who you are."

Vikki leaned her head on Jeremy's shoulder, and he pulled

her close. Finally, she straightened herself and said, "I probably should go now."

"Yeah, probably." His eyes held a conflicting message as she lifted her head for his kiss.

"I don't want to, though."

He ran his fingers up through the back of her hair and met her lips again. "And I'd love to beg you to stay, but..."

Vikki gave him a shy smile and stood up. "Bye, Jeremy, I'll see you later." Then she walked through the door before he could change his mind.

Jeremy got ready for work, wondering how he would be able to concentrate during his shift.

CHAPTER TWENTY-THREE

Lee had been agitated earlier after the church service when Jeremy had prevented his plans to speak to Brandon. He'd watched that lame associate pastor knock and gain entrance into Brandon's office. Brandon had shut the door behind him, indicating it was a meeting of some significance. He worried that Vikki might have talked to Jeremy about their encounter Saturday at school. He might have been a little too rough on Vikki trying to scare her. It may have backfired. Jeremy might now be relating his threats against Vikki to Brandon. It didn't matter. Even if she had told Jeremy everything, Lee had ammunition against any accusations Vikki might make. He would fight fire with fire.

As Lee sat in the oversized leather recliner in his home office, he delighted in the pictures he held in his hand. The photos had captured Jeremy and Jordan holding beer cans and prancing around with the girls. Of course, the most damaging one was the image of that troublemaker, Vikki, sitting astride their esteemed preacher. He leaned his head back and chuckled. The pictures had been a godsend—

completely unexpected, but they would come in handy indeed.

He had wondered, at the time, if hiring a private detective to follow Vikki was over the top. He had wanted to convince her that he wasn't a man to mess with, so she would keep her mouth shut. The plan was to scare her with pictures of places she had been, to prove he was watching her, and to convince her he meant business. Now, he was glad he made that decision. These bonus pictures would prove priceless.

Lee smirked as he flipped through the pictures putting the three incriminating Jeremy on top of the pile. He would take them to Brandon in the morning. Brandon trusted him. These snapshots of Jeremy tossing back beer and partying would discredit their new associate pastor's character and cast doubt on any allegations that Vikki may have made about Lee abusing his wife.

It did bother him that Jeremy's sister, Jessie, and Vikki were friends. Would they trade stories, make any connections? It was doubtful that Jessie would say anything about her fling with him, but if Vikki took Jessie into her confidence about his wife's injuries, Jessie might reveal their one-night stand and his betrayal of Lisa.

Getting Jeremy fired would solve all his problems. Vikki would leave with him, and he was sure Jessie would go also. He leaned forward, his elbows on the arms of the chair, deep in thought. A hesitant knock on the door startled him. "What?" he asked with annoyance.

"Supper's ready." The voice was as hesitant as the knock.

He grudgingly pulled himself out of the chair, stomped to the door, and opened it.

"Bring my dinner in here tonight," he said brusquely. "I'm busy." Lisa looked like a whipped pup but was silent as she walked into the kitchen to get the plates.

A sudden idea prompted Lee to follow her. "On second

thought, I think I will eat in the dining room with you." He really should make up with his wife. There was still a chance that Vikki would make trouble for him, and he was afraid Lisa's father was getting suspicious, especially with her broken arm. Lisa needed to be on his side. His future success depended on it. In a few years, Lisa's father would retire, and Lee would become a senior partner in the firm. Then he could divorce Lisa if something better caught his eye. He was never that invested in their relationship. She had been a means to an end for him. Not that he had it so bad. Lisa was attractive, even with the few extra pounds she had put on. Besides, he knew there were always other women who were available to him without jeopardizing his marriage.

* * *

Lisa and Lee ate dinner in silence. As they were finishing the meal, Lee reached for her hand across the table,

"You know, Lisa, I'm really sorry about that arm," Lee's voice was remorseful. He sat with his elbows on the table and sported a sorrowful look. "I know I've lost my temper with you at times, but you've got to believe me about this. I honestly didn't mean to push you down the stairs. I was trying to talk to you, but I tripped and fell. If you could just try not to make me so angry. You know my job gets me all tensed up." He got up and knelt beside her chair. "I love you, sweetheart," he said in a contrite tone.

Anger and a flame of hope clashed within Lisa's heart as she forced herself to look at him. She wanted to believe that he cared, yet she'd been deceived by declarations of love and empty promises countless times before. And she knew he had indeed pushed her down the stairs—hadn't he?

"Come on, Lisa," he pleaded, "Give me another chance."

She flinched at his touch and squeezed her fingers into a fist. He pulled her out of the chair. "Let's go talk on the couch."

She trudged alongside Lee. He was putting more effort into persuading her this time. Usually, he just apologized and then waited for a few days until the incident blew over. Then again, he had been more violent these past few weeks. His verbal abuse and shoves had escalated into a more sinister variety of violence.

"I know what you'd like," he said. "Remember those black pearls my secretary wore to last year's Christmas party. You commented on how beautiful they were." His voice was syrupy sweet as he turned her toward him. "We'll go to the jewelry store this week and pick out a strand." His hand caressed her arm, and he kissed her cheek.

Lisa stared at him, attempting to decide if he was trying to buy her forgiveness or silence. Her stomach churned when she remembered the crazed anger Lee had shown toward Vikki just a few days ago. Was he afraid Vikki would end up telling Jeremy or even calling the police? Hopelessness entangled Lisa, and she didn't know how to free herself. She forced a smile. "Okay, that would be fine." Black pearls were a luxury that would make most of Lisa's friends envious.

"Good," he said with the air of closing a business deal and gave her another peck on the cheek. After dinner, he returned to his office. "I'll go get some more work done now."

* * *

The small brass lamp on Lisa's nightstand cast just enough light to reveal the beautiful furniture that decorated the room. Lisa had been thrilled with their bedroom when she and Lee first moved into their new house in Majestic Meadows, the most prestigious place to live in Claymon. Lee had hired an interior decorator with specific instructions indicating the elegant and professional type of atmosphere he wanted his home to display except for one room. He had allowed Lisa full sway in the decorating of the master bedroom. She had chosen quality pine furniture and a luxurious cream carpet. The shades of mauve and cream in the bedspread, curtains, and chair exuded a lovely, sophisticated appeal. Now though, as she lay in her lonely bed, the beautiful room was a façade, a reflection of how artificial her life had become.

Lee had gone out for a "couple of drinks" with his lawyer buddies, a pastime he kept hidden from everyone at church. Lisa knew he would probably be out until two a.m. or later and then go to the office late as he often did on Monday mornings. She also knew that there was a strong possibility that his evening's activities would include women, and Lee might even take one of them to a motel for a meaningless fling. At least that's what he called them. He needed the excitement of these little affairs to relieve all his anxiety, he explained to her, because of the extreme pressures he faced at work. His indiscretions were also a secret, of course. Other people, especially those from church, wouldn't understand the stress his career caused him.

Lies and secrets were the essence of Lisa's life with Lee. The Bannisters were an elite family in the community. They chose their friends and social activities with care to reflect their prominent position, and Lee strove with relentless zeal to maintain that image. He even took a leadership position in the church as an outward show of integrity. No one could ever discover that he was involved in affairs or abused his wife.

Lisa accepted that Lee engaged in extramarital activities occasionally as long as they were one-night stands and never involved an employee or friend. As long as there was no emotional involvement on Lee's part, she could tolerate it, knowing he valued his future with the law firm enough that he would not end the marriage.

However, one of the women Lee had a fling with had called Lisa about four years ago. She told Lisa she worked in the office. Lee had tried to convince Lisa that the girl was lying, that she was an angry employee trying to blackmail him over being let go. Lisa didn't believe his story. She had blown up over the office affair, and Lee had promised to straighten up and quit cheating altogether. She thought he had been faithful for a while.

Eventually, though, signs he had gone back to his old ways began to appear. Clues like phone numbers in his bill-fold, late nights at the computer, messages on his cell phone from women she didn't know, and bills from florists, indicated that he was unfaithful again. Lisa knew Lee would keep his reputation untainted regardless of the lies he would need to tell or measures he had to employ. She was troubled over his increasing anger lately, especially his outburst against Vikki. Lee couldn't afford Vikki divulging his secrets to Jeremy or anyone else, and the thought that she might expose the truth terrified Lisa.

Why did she put up with the lies, abuse, and affairs? That was the million-dollar question, and she didn't know the answer. As an only child, Lisa had been a source of disappointment for her father. He had wanted a son to inherit his law practice, but his diabetic wife couldn't become pregnant again for health reasons, and he never considered Lisa to be lawyer material.

Her mother died from complications of her disease when Lisa was thirteen, and her father had remarried a much younger woman who had no desire, or time, to raise a child. His new wife's interests ran more along the lines of the monetary benefits Lisa's father could provide. Her step-mother and her busy father paid little attention to Lisa. As long as she kept her grades up and stayed out of the kind of trouble that might embarrass her parents, she had pretty much free rein, though what she longed for was her father's love.

Lisa remembered her intense yearning for someone to pay attention to her as a child. She sought her father's approval by attempting to become whoever he wanted her to be, but she could never quite measure up to his expectations. As a teenager, her lack of confidence and less-than-perfect figure was a constant source of irritation for her father, who nagged her about losing weight so she could catch a wealthy and ambitious husband.

Lisa's musings led her back to the first time she had met Lee. Her father introduced him to her as the most promising new lawyer in town. Lee's handsome face and tall stature pleased Lisa, and she was flattered when he asked her out.

Lee's father was a prominent businessman in Claymon who owned a sporting goods store and the local theatre. His family was well known and respected in the community. Lisa's father persuaded her that Lee would be the perfect husband, and with him as a partner in the law firm, she would never lack material things or social status. He also approved of her teaching career because it was good for a lawyer to have a professional wife. Her father had finally found her acceptable.

Yet, Lee's interest was somewhat of a surprise to her. She had never considered herself attractive to men and had dated only a few times. She felt pretty, though, when she was with him. He could have any girl he wanted, but for some reason, he chose her. When he proposed, she gladly accepted, and for the first few months of her marriage, he treated her well. She soon learned, however, that he needed to control everything in his life, including her. She had accepted his domineering

behavior when they dated as being characteristic of a confident and influential man. In public, he showered her with
attention and was the perfect gentleman, so when he got
angry and belittled her in private, she chalked it up to stress
from work.

As the pressures and responsibilities at work increased,
so did his demands on her. When Jennifer came along, Lisa
was absorbed with her care, and Lee became even more
controlling and verbally abusive. His attitude and behavior
followed a pattern of verbal abuse, apologies, and better
treatment for a time, and then the verbal abuse would esca-
late again. Months turned into years, and the abuse went
from verbal put-downs to pushing and shoving. It had
become a way of life, and in the past few years, he had even
hit Lisa occasionally. Then would come the apologies, blam-
ing, and promises—all a study in deception and shattered
dreams.

The few times she had threatened to leave, he had ratch-
eted up the insults and launched into a tirade. He claimed she
was trash, blamed her for causing him to lose his temper, and
insisted he would never let her leave because he planned to
inherit her father's business. He ranted about how she would
lose everything, even their daughter, because he knew the
right people and could win custody. He had already spread
rumors around the church and his office that she was not
mentally well, and truthfully, she even questioned her sanity
at times. Just tonight, she had sold her self-worth for a strand
of black pearls. She was in a vicious cycle, a hamster on a
wheel, and she didn't know how to escape it.

CHAPTER TWENTY-FOUR

A sense of apprehension, vague and distant at the onset, swept over Vikki as she prepared for bed. Unable to put a name to it, she dismissed it as an after-effect of an evening laced with emotion. Now, though, as she lay in bed, the feeling permeated her thoughts. She wrestled with it through the night as it invaded her dreams, urging her to an action she could not discern.

As Vikki dressed for work the following morning, the feeling became a directive: *Talk to Brandon about Lee as soon as possible*. Shaken, she felt compelled to follow it. She decided not to inform Jeremy of her change of plans. He would only worry and try to talk her into waiting until he could come along.

It was 6:30 a.m., early enough that no one would be in the church office. Thankfully, the answering machine picked up, so she didn't have to speak to anyone. She left a message and hoped Brandon would get back to her soon.

* * *

Jordan stood up from his desk and stretched his arms over his head. It had been an uneventful early morning, giving him time to catch up on some paperwork. He walked to the fire station's common area and found Jeremy sitting on the couch reading his Bible and writing notes, probably working on next week's sermon. "Hey, Preacher Boy," he said as he plopped on the chair across from the couch. "You got a minute?"

"Sure. I'm just killing time. It's kind of quiet around here today." He couldn't concentrate anyway; his head was still swimming with the events of the night before. He closed his Bible and slid it with his papers on the couch.

"Yeah, it is kind of slow today. That's good though." Jordan shifted in his seat.

Jeremy's face questioned him.

"Jessie and I are getting married," Jordan spouted.

Surprise swept across Jeremy's face. "Married? Wow." He paused, unsure how to continue. "Anytime soon?"

"Well, I wanted this Saturday, but Jessie thinks she needs more time."

Jeremy misunderstood Jordan's wisecrack. A sudden thought whacked him in the gut. "Do you have to? I mean Jessie's not…"

Jordan's grin vanished. "Hey, don't even go there. It's not a shotgun wedding."

"Sorry, Jordan. It just seems so sudden. You haven't known each other that long." He smiled slowly. "I think it's great, man, really." And he did think it was great. Jordan was a good Christian man, a perfect match for his strong-willed sister.

"Thanks." He met Jeremy's gaze. "I've prayed for God to bring someone into my life for a long time. I know we haven't known each other long, but I also know it's right." He tilted his head. "I was hoping you'd give me your blessing."

"Of course I do." Jeremy's eyes sparkled. "You know, of course," he said with amusement, "This means we'll be brothers."

Jordan feigned a grimace. "Oh, yeah. Well, there's always a downside."

At that moment, the shrill alarm split the calmness of the morning. Jeremy sprinted to his rig and pulled on his turnout gear, his heart pounding. He met Jordan at the ambulance, and they tore out of the station, racing to a house fire. Jeremy would have his first chance to fight a large fire as a certified firefighter and EMT. Adrenaline rushed through his body creating a mix of trepidation and excitement, and the realization that all his training would be put to use.

Smoke billowed from an abandoned house in the old downtown area of Claymon. Firefighters broke the windows to ventilate the building. Jeremy and another firefighter battled smoke so thick they couldn't see their hands in front of them as they searched for any people that might have wandered into the deserted house. As they stumbled through the darkness, Jeremy lifted a silent prayer that there would be no one trapped inside and that they wouldn't find someone who had succumbed to the smoke. They searched the house until they were sure it was empty.

After confirming that there were no people in the house, the main concern was preventing the fire from spreading to nearby dwellings. Three hours later, after shoveling cinders and tossing out anything that might burn to prevent rekindling, the weary firefighters returned to the station. They all took quick showers and ate a late lunch.

Jordan looked Jeremy up after a required training session later that afternoon. "You performed well today. I could tell you were really pumped."

Jeremy perched on the edge of his bunk. "Yeah, it was

pretty exhilarating. I'm just glad no one was injured or worse. I'm not sure I'd respond properly."

"Why?" Jordan gave him a puzzled look. "I've seen you work with injured people before, and I have a lot of faith in your ability."

Jeremy's eyes shadowed. "I'm always concerned about it. I just don't want to be helpless in a situation. I don't want to let anyone down, or not be able to…" his voice trailed off. "Anyway," he continued attempting a smile, "It was exciting, and I was able to handle everything."

Jordan spun a chair around and straddled it, facing Jeremy. "You're afraid you won't be able to save someone?" he finished Jeremy's thoughts. "Hey," he swept the room with his hand. "There's not a person in this place who hasn't known that fear. And it will happen. Someone will be severely injured, or even die, and you won't be able to prevent it."

"I know." Jeremy rested back on his arms. "I've tried to prepare for that."

Jordan leaned forward, linking his arms across the back of the chair. "But it's more personal with you, isn't it?" he asked quietly. He ventured on, watching Jeremy's reaction. "Jessie told me about Shannon's death."

Jeremy averted his eyes and sucked in his breath. "Oh."

"Don't be angry with Jessie. I asked her to tell me because I felt there was something traumatic connected with the way Shannon died." His voice was sober. "I only brought it up because I think you need to deal with your fears. You can't let them interfere with your ability to react appropriately on this job," he finished.

Jeremy caught his eyes. "It's ok. I'm finally dealing with my emotions actually," he said with measured words. "I met with Brandon yesterday, and he helped me realize I needed to let go of my guilt and anger. It was painful and frightening." He bit the insides of his cheeks. "I fell apart." His eyes clouded, and he waited until he could trust his voice. "It's a difficult process, but I'm making progress." His face was pensive. "I do fear my ability to handle losing someone, though, or not being able to stop something terrible from happening."

"Those are normal fears, Jeremy. Maybe they are a little more intense for you. But I have confidence in your ability to handle any situation you might face." Jordan held Jeremy's eyes. "There was nothing you could have done to save Shannon. You know that, don't you? You were outnumbered and unarmed. Nobody could have fought off those guys."

Jeremy shook his head and blew out a puff of air. "I don't know. I'll always wonder if I could have done something different. I've relived it over and over," his voice was barely a whisper. "But thanks."

Jordan frowned and shook his head. "I doubt it, and I'm not sure reliving it is helpful. Do you ever think about those guys? I mean," he looked away and shrugged, "I can't imagine how hard that would be, you know just knowing."

Jeremy closed his eyes for a second before answering. "Not a whole lot. Until recently, I spent most of my energy denying my emotions. Brandon and I touched on the subject, but it will take time." He cast his eyes to the side, "That's for sure."

"Well, I'm glad Brandon is counseling you. Guilt and bitterness will wreck you, but you are a strong person and a great firefighter." Jordan winked, "And not too shabby as a preacher."

Jeremy laughed, got to his feet, and tapped Jordan's arm as he walked away. "I do appreciate your confidence in me."

"By the way, Preacher Boy," Jordan called after him, "About our conversation earlier this morning."

Jeremy stopped and looked over his shoulder. "Yeah?" He started back toward Jordan.

"You really ought to have some confidence in me too, you know."

"How's that?"

"Jessie and I aren't sleeping together. I'm as pure as a choir boy." His grin was mischievous.

Jeremy flashed him an incredulous smile and shook his head. "See to it you stay that way."

"Will do, Preacher," he winked. "Actually, I'm kinda worried about your behavior."

"What are you talking about?"

"Ah, come on now, I've seen the way you turn to putty every time Vikki looks at you with those sexy green eyes," Jordan said as he fluttered his eyelashes. "And furthermore," he continued with mock seriousness, "I think you enjoyed your wrestling match with her at the concert just a little too much." Jordan punched him lightly. "When are you going to admit you are in love with her?"

Jeremy returned his punch, "Ok, I give up." He held his hands up. "I admit it. I'm in love with Vikki," he said to Jordan's wide-eyed stare. "Just so you know, I told her last night. And yes, as a matter of fact, I did enjoy our little 'wrestling match.'"

Jordan dropped his jaw and let out a laugh, "That's great, Jeremy. I'm really happy for you. But, hey," he tossed back as he sauntered off, "No more wrestling matches until you're married."

* * *

Brandon's look was intense as he observed the pictures Lee had tossed on his desk, giving special attention to the photo of Jeremy and Jordan with the beer cans held up in the air and the one with Vikki sitting on top of Jeremy. Brandon frowned at the arrogant man sitting across from him, one who wore an "I told you so" look and seemed a bit too eager for him to condemn their new pastor.

"Tell me, Lee, where did you get these pictures?"

Lee scowled. "Why does it matter?" he snapped, annoyance coloring his tone. "You can see the kind of hypocrite our associate minister is. He hides behind his fake integrity."

Brandon tugged at his chin. "Vikki left me a message on my phone this morning." He observed Lee closely. "She told me you would be bringing me some unflattering photos of Jeremy. As a matter of fact, I'm meeting with her this evening."

Lee blanched but didn't speak.

"She also said that you had someone follow her and take pictures while she was at a concert."

"So what if I did?" Lee leaned forward, his face tight with anger, his voice haughty. "Maybe I know things about Vikki that you don't. I can tell you this. A minister has no business hanging out with the likes of her or that sister of his, drinking and partying at some rock concert." His fist struck Brandon's desk. "I want Jeremy out of our church, the sooner the better," he demanded.

Brandon's eyebrows knitted together. "What's this really about, Lee?" He kept his voice low but firm. "I'll certainly talk to Jeremy about the pictures, but why did you tell Vikki about them? Why would you have someone follow her?" He raised his hands with palms up. "What am I missing here?"

Lee dove across the desk and grabbed the photos from Brandon's hands. "Never mind," he fumed, "I'll show them to the other elders. We'll just see what they have to say." He headed for the door, but then he spun around and flung the pictures on Brandon's desk. "I have plenty of copies. Why don't you spend a little time studying them?" he said with scorn. "Maybe you'll change your mind about who you have preaching in our church." With that, he stormed out of the office, slamming the door behind him.

Brandon gaped in astonishment at Lee's outburst. What had gotten into him? Was he a man prone to beating his wife, as Vikki asserted? He could hardly fathom Lee capable of such violence, but neither could he deny the anger Lee had just displayed or the bizarre way he had Vikki followed. Did Lee know Vikki was suspicious of his actions concerning his wife? Did he believe Jeremy led a double life? And was that a possibility? Lee had never favored Jeremy being hired for the New Life Community position as a pastor, claiming he was too young and inexperienced. Brandon guessed the real reason was that Lee felt threatened by Jeremy's approach to preaching the Word and his enthusiasm for the congregation to live what they believed or "walk the talk," as he put it. He didn't think Lee wasn't all that excited about accountability.

Brandon sat at his desk with his hands clasped. Were Lee's actions simply a ploy to get Jeremy fired, or did his motives run deeper? The pictures were provocative enough to raise some questions. At least Lee seemed to think so. Was Lee desperate to get Vikki out of the way because of her allegations about him beating his wife, assuming she would leave if Jeremy were relieved of his job at the church? He sighed. Perhaps he would learn more at this afternoon's appointment with Vikki. Her tone had sounded frightened in the message, and she claimed it was urgent they meet today.

* * *

Vikki's distraction had made it challenging to teach her class. She'd received confirmation that Brandon would meet with her at 4:30. Time seemed to drag by, yet she wasn't eager for the end of the school day. Not caring for confrontation in general, she dreaded her meeting with Brandon this evening.

Lisa kept her distance during the day, choosing to eat her lunch in her room instead of the lounge. Vikki was sure Lisa didn't want to answer questions about her broken arm. Her avoidance was a blessing since Vikki wasn't keen on engaging in conversations that might lead to places she didn't care to go to today.

Vikki began the drive to the church feeling nervous about her meeting with Pastor Brandon. She became aware of a car in her rearview mirror. Any other time, she would have thought nothing of it, but after learning that someone had followed her the other night, she was very conscious of any vehicle traveling behind her.

Gray clouds obscured the late afternoon sun causing it to seem later than it was. The car following her hung back far enough that she couldn't make out the driver. It trailed her to the main highway leading into Claymon and turned right as she did. Her stomach flipped, sending pinpricks of fear up her arms. She felt sure the car was tailing her. Was Lee, or the person who had followed her to the concert, driving the vehicle this evening? She made an unexpected turn onto a side road to test her theory, and the car behind her followed. She turned on another road that led back to the highway; her pursuer did the same. Shock pulsed through her veins, confirming her suspicions. Someone was indeed following her.

Panic rippled through Vikki, and her stomach leaped. Her hands shook as she clenched the steering wheel, continuing until she could merge onto the interstate that would take her to Indianapolis and in the opposite direction of Claymon. She would try to lose her pursuer on the highway. As she frantically steered her car down the ramp, the driver of the other car drew up on her right side, crowding her and causing her to swerve abruptly into the lane of oncoming traffic. Terror seized her. She jammed her foot to the floorboard and flew in front of a car in the right lane. Driven by near hysteria, she wove in and out of the traffic, afraid to look in her mirror. She zoomed down the interstate at speeds nearing ninety miles an hour, nearly losing control of her vehicle at one point. *Where were the cops when you needed them?*

Spying an exit ahead, Vikki decided to make her break. Waiting until the last possible minute, she took a leap of faith, zipped across two lanes of traffic, and veered onto the ramp. As she approached the road the ramp connected with, she stole a glance in her rearview mirror. No one.was behind her. The car swerved as she jammed on the brakes, her tires screeching to a stop at the intersection. Her pursuer no longer on her tail, she slowed to a safer speed. Whoever was following her wouldn't guess where she was going. She tried to calm herself enough to think clearly about her next move. Heading for the exit that would take her back to Claymon, she considered driving to a police station or her parents' house but instead traveled to the church, determined to complete her mission.

With her heart still pounding, she drove into the parking lot. She pulled into a parking space next to a car she hoped was Brandon's, released her death grip on the steering wheel and covered her face. Her hands trembled as they supported her bowed head, and her legs shook so hard she wondered if they would hold her up. Vikki debated whether to leave her vehicle's safety or give up the whole idea and head for home, but decided she had come this far and was afraid to go home anyway. Vikki bounded out of her car, locked the door, and bolted to the entrance.

* * *

Hearing the door open, Brandon met his visibly shaken visitor. "What in the world is the matter, Vikki?"

"Someone followed me and tried to run me off the road. I'm pretty sure it was Lee," she gasped, sucking air.

Brandon steadied her with his arm and spoke quietly. "You're ok, now. Try to take deep breaths." He waited until she calmed somewhat. "Did he follow you here?"

"No, I don't think so," she panted, "I outran him on the interstate. I think I lost him." Her eyes were so large, Brandon wondered if they might pop out of their sockets. "He forced me onto the highway right in front of another car and then chased me until I was able to find an exit and lose him."

He took her elbow and led her to his office. "Come in and sit down. Tell me what this is all about."

Vikki sat on the edge of the chair across from Brandon, seated at his desk. Her voice wobbled, but her words were unmistakable. "Lee beats his wife. He broke her arm. When I walked in on him abusing her Saturday at school, he threatened that he would beat Lisa until I wouldn't recognize her and destroy Jeremy's career if I told anyone." She stopped, catching her breath. "I didn't know what to do, but I can't ignore it any longer."

Shock played on Brandon's features. He could no longer disregard the charges against Lee and, looking back, it all fell into place. He was embarrassed as he remembered his condescending attitude when Jeremy told him a few weeks ago of Vikki's accusations about Lee. He also recalled his conversation with Lee the next day when he spoke of his wife's mental problems and how he was afraid that "his associate minister's girlfriend" had misunderstood the situation. Moreover, Jeremy had mentioned yesterday that Vikki was upset about a problem at school. He had meant to question him further, but their conversation had taken another path. Brandon's voice was solemn. "Vikki, Lee was in here this afternoon with the pictures you left the message about. He also admitted having you followed, but I'm still not sure why."

"I didn't see the pictures clearly," Vikki remarked. "I know he took them when we were at the concert, but I'm not sure what they are."

"They're pictures of Jeremy and his friend, Jordan, drinking beer and dancing in a suggestive way with you and another girl who I believe is Jeremy's sister," Brandon explained, pushing the pictures across the table to her. "They appear to be having a good time," he asserted.

Vikki's mouth fell open in surprise as she took in the pictures, and it occurred to her that the situation would be comical under other circumstances. "Jeremy and Jordan weren't drinking. Those were just cans they found on the ground." She wrinkled her brow. "Whoever took the picture must have had a telescopic lens."

Brandon scrunched his eyebrows and gazed at the pictures. "But they have the cans up close to their mouths. It certainly looks like they are drinking and swaggering around."

Vikki cocked her head and gave him a look. "They were fooling around, that's all. Those were empty cans Jordan found on the ground. It was just a joke. Nobody was drinking. You can ask any of us."

"Well," he sighed. "It's a joke that has stirred up a hornet's nest. I'm quite sure Lee has contacted the other elders by now. Here's another one." He gave his head a slight shake and pursed his lips. "It sure looks like you were all having a good time."

Vikki's eyes rounded, and her cheeks grew pink as she peered at the picture of her sitting on top of Jeremy. "We were acting silly, that's all."

Brandon grew rigid as a thought occurred to him. "You think Lee tried to run you off the road?"

"Somebody sure did. I'm assuming it was Lee. I never did get a good look at the driver." She stiffened. "Why?"

Brandon's expression was telling. "Did Lee know I was coming to see you?" she rasped.

"I mentioned it to him this morning." He hesitated. "Vikki, be careful and try to lay low for a while. Lee may be desperate enough to harm you if he thinks you told me about his abusing Lisa."

Vikki shuddered. "Lee tried to run me into oncoming traffic to keep me from seeing you." Her voice was shaky. "I could have been killed."

"I'm sorry, Vikki. I should have never mentioned that you had a meeting with me." He hung his head. "I had no idea he would attempt to stop our meeting. I was a fool to dismiss Jeremy's words when we met at the restaurant."

The green of Vikki's eyes was vivid against her pale skin. "You couldn't have known, but I'm afraid of what he might do to Lisa tonight."

Brandon looked thoughtful. "You know, I don't think Lee will do anything tonight, especially if he thinks you talked to me. I would think he'd be on his best behavior as far as his wife is concerned." He brought his fist to his mouth. "I tell you what. I'll give him a call tonight and tell him I want to talk more about the pictures. He might cool off a little if he thinks I'm listening to him. That might get his mind off of you."

Vikki nodded, "And help Lisa, too."

"I don't think you should be alone. Is Jeremy at the fire station tonight?"

"Yes, he's working the overnight shift."

Brandon hesitated. "Maybe I should follow you home and

go inside to check things out. Are you sure Lee didn't follow you here?"

"Yes, I lost him on the highway. I don't think anyone followed me after that."

"I imagine that he thinks he scared you away from seeing me, but we can't be too sure. Let me follow you home just in case." He paused, "I would ask you to stay the night at my house, but Alice is away visiting her sister. You could still come if you feel comfortable with that."

"No, that's ok. I will ask Jessie to stay with me." Vikki texted Jessie right then, asking her to spend the night because she was uneasy being alone and would explain later. Jessie texted back immediately with yes; she would be there in thirty minutes.

"I think it will be fine with both of us there, but I would like you to follow me home if it isn't too much trouble, I mean."

The slightest hint of a grin tugged at Brandon's mouth. No wonder Jeremy was enamored with her. She was a breath of fresh air, charming and unassuming, a stark contrast to the petty, self-righteous people who often sat across from him in his office. "It's no problem. I promise. You have my number. Call if you are at all concerned, and I will be there. I will check on you in a few hours."

* * *

Lee waited to drive to the church until he knew Vikki would be there if she decided to keep her meeting with Brandon. He moved to the edge of the lot to look for her car, then swore and cuffed the steering wheel when he saw it parked right next to Brandon's. That wild goose chase she had taken him on was a clever ploy to lose him, but she couldn't have been aware that he knew she was meeting with Brandon. Lee gripped the steering wheel so hard his knuckles turned white. He wanted to scare her away, but that hadn't worked because here she was. She was probably telling Brandon everything, including him trying to run her off the road. Cursing, he drove out of the parking lot. He needed to think. He must scare Vikki into silence as he had done with Jessie. Jessie was frightened enough to keep quiet, at least for now. It was possible, though, that Vikki would confide in Jessie about her suspicions. If they began to compare notes, well then, he would stand to lose a lot, far too much. Both of them must be silenced, but Lee wasn't sure how to accomplish that. On an impulse, he drove toward Vikki's home.

As he approached the farmhouse, he saw a grassy area to the right of the garage just beyond several rows of trees. A barely visible path that must have once been an old driveway led to a border of trees where he could park and be out of view as he waited for Vikki to return. He wasn't sure of his plans, but he had to find some way to scare her off, and it wouldn't hurt to spy a little.

CHAPTER TWENTY-FIVE

Brandon followed Vikki home, checked the house, and then waited on the porch until Jessie arrived. He greeted her then addressed Vikki, "Please be sure to let me know if anything appears out of the ordinary, no matter what the time."

Confusion played on Jessie's features as Vikki agreed. "What is going on?"

"Vikki will tell you about it. I think you should go inside and stay put for the evening." As he walked down the drive, Brandon looked back and held up his finger. "I'll check with you in a couple of hours."

The girls stepped into the house, and Vikki locked the door. "What is going on?" Jessie repeated.

"Come sit at the table and I'll tell you." Vikki motioned for Jessie to sit and positioned herself across the table. "I went to see Brandon about some issues with a man at church."

"Is that why you wanted me to come over? Are you scared of this guy?"

"Yes, but I don't know how much I should tell you. I don't want to involve you in something that might be dangerous."

"For heaven's sake, I think you need to if you are too afraid to stay alone," Jessie pressed.

Vikki sat paralyzed with indecision as anger, fear and hopelessness clouded her mind. Jessie touched her hand, and her tone softened, "Please tell me. Maybe I can help."

Vikki took a deep breath and began sharing her encounters with Lee at school and church. She explained about Lee beating his wife and his warnings about her telling anyone. She told Jessie about the pictures he took of the four of them at the concert and ended with the evening's events. "I planned to meet with Brandon to tell him about Lee and to let him know that Lee had unflattering pictures of Jeremy." Her words were rapid as she relayed the part about Lee following her and running her off the road. "I just don't know what to do next and I'm afraid," she finished.

Jessie's face conveyed her shock. She shook her head in disbelief. "I think there is something you need to know." She clasped her hands together, "I hate to tell you, but I think it may help you nail this creep."

Vikki stared at her friend, "What are you talking about? Tell me what?"

Jessie cast a regretful look at Vikki and began. "You may have second thoughts about being my friend after I tell you, but here goes."

Jessie's sordid story of her relationship with Lee Bannister, their implausible meeting at church, and his threatening phone call blew Vikki away. She could tell how it hurt Jessie to share it with her.

"That's unbelievable and sad, but it doesn't change our friendship. You were young. We all make mistakes." She patted Jessie's hand. "Jordan told Jeremy you were upset after meeting Lee at church, but he only said that you used to work with Lee and had a falling out."

Jessie nodded. "I told Jordan the whole story, but it must

have been after he talked to Jeremy. No one knows the story except you and Jordan now. I guess I will need to tell Jeremy."

"That's your choice. It's not for me to tell anyone."

"Thanks, Vikki. I do want to confide in him, but no one else has a reason to know. Except," she said, her eyes widening, "It might help you persuade your pastor if he knew more about Lee's character. Should we tell him?"

Vikki considered the question. "I think we should and the sooner the better. He won't need to know any details, but it would help our case. I'm sorry that it will put you in a bad position, but I am not feeling very safe now. What if Lee finds out we have shared information? He may have even followed us here."

"I agree. Should we call Brandon?"

Vikki thought for a minute, "Maybe we should text and say we are coming over. I'd rather tell him in person."

* * *

Lee had waited for over a half-hour and his impatience was growing. Maybe Vikki wasn't coming home after all. He might have frightened her enough that she would stay with someone else. He would wait a few minutes longer. Just then, two cars approached the drive and turned in. Anxiety clutched him as he watched to see who had followed Vikki home. As they walked into the light shed by the lamp on the garage door, Vikki and Brandon's forms came into view. He couldn't hear them, but it seemed Brandon had escorted Vikki home. They went inside for a few minutes and then came out and sat on the porch swing. Lee froze, not sure what to do. While he was considering his actions, a third car pulled in the driveway. He watched as someone emerged from the vehicle carrying a backpack. It was Jessie! And it looked like she was spending the night. He watched as

Brandon left the two women. Now he was sure that they would talk and figure out their shared connection to him.

He tapped his forehead rapidly, trying to formulate a plan. He would wait here for a while to see if anything else happened, then perhaps he'd make another call to Jessie, to tell her he knew she had talked to Vikki and warn her to back off or there would be tragic consequences.

After another thirty minutes, Lee decided to place the warning call to Jessie. As he scanned his contact list, he saw the door open, and the two girls hurried to Jessie's car. He wondered if Jessie was leaving for the night, but Vikki hopped in the passenger's side, and they took off down the driveway. Where would they be going at this time of night? He waited until they turned onto the street, then slowly started down the driveway, waiting to flip on his headlights until he turned onto the road.

CHAPTER TWENTY-SIX

Brandon had replied to Vikki's text immediately, given his address, and told them to be careful. He suggested that they drive Jessie's car so that if Lee were hanging around the roads close to Vikki's house, he wouldn't recognize the vehicle. They were quiet as they journeyed down the dark country road. Suddenly, Jessie stiffened and gripped the steering wheel.

"What is it?" asked Vikki, noticing Jessie's eyes trained on the rearview mirror.

"Oh, there is a car behind us, but it's probably nothing. I'm just a little jumpy, I guess."

Vikki looked in her side-view mirror as the car gained on them. Her stomach churned at the sight of the approaching vehicle. "Jessie, I think we're being followed."

The car sped up and flashed its lights at them. "Call the police!" Jessie shouted.

Vikki had already acted. "Jeremy's at the fire station. I'm calling him now."

Jessie maintained her speed, "How do I get to Brandon's?" she shouted.

"Stay on this road until we get to the stop sign, then turn left. It's a few miles from here."

"Hello, Vikki?" Jeremy answered.

"Someone is following us. I think it's Lee." Vikki's voice rose with each word.

"What? Where are you?"

"On my road, driving to Brandon's."

A jolt caused Vikki to drop her phone as Lee's car tapped Jessie's. Jessie floored it and the car flew down the road, kicking up gravel behind it. Lee caught up to them and again bumped them on the side. Jessie tried to steer as they skidded across the road, barely missing a telephone pole. She swerved and ran nose down into a ditch as Lee's car streaked ahead. Jessie shoved the gear shift in reverse, but the wheels spun in the dirt. She tried again with the same result. They were stuck.

For a second, the girls sat in stunned silence. Then Vikki grabbed her phone. "We've gotta get out of here. I'm sure that was Lee. He may come back."

"Vikki, where are you? Speak to me!" came Jeremy's distraught voice from the phone.

"We're in a ditch, on my road, running toward trees."

"Vikki, wait! Who's with you?"

"Jessie," she yelled, disconnected, and pocketed the phone in her jacket.

They ran through the rough field, tripping over the left-over stubble of harvest, to a group of trees that would provide them some cover, then navigated as quickly as they could through the darkness, stumbling over tree roots and trying to keep an eye on the road as they ran.

Lee's car screeched to a halt, made a U-turn, and headed back to where his quarry had spun into a ditch. He spied them, running across open land toward a wooded area. Smirking, he returned to his car and drove to the next road planning to cut them off where they would emerge from the trees.

* * *

"Jordan!" Jeremy shouted. "Lee is chasing Vikki and Jessie in her car. They've wrecked near Vikki's house."

Jordan alerted his superiors that he was on an emergency call and sprinted toward the garage. "I'm with you, Jeremy. Get in the ambulance!" Jordan mouthed a quick prayer for God's intervention as he and Jeremy jumped into the emergency vehicle.

Jordan drove rapidly without turning on the siren until he approached Vikki's road and caught sight of a car off the road. It couldn't be Vikki's, though; this one was red. He sprang from the rescue vehicle and sprinted down to the ditch. "It's Jessie's car!"

Jordan quickly scanned the interior of the car. "They may have run across the field to hide if they weren't caught by Lee first. I'm going to drive up to the next road to see if they are walking on the street. Do you want to run ahead and check it out?"

Jeremy was already racing across the field with a first aid bag in hand. "On my way," he yelled.

Jordan drove slowly, looking for signs of the two girls or any vehicle on the road, but saw nothing. Doubting they could have gone any further, he pulled into the next street, planning to turn around and head back toward Jessie's vehicle. As Jordan made his turn, he noticed a car pulled off to the side of the road a short distance away, and he went to investigate.

* * *

Lee had parked about twenty feet from the grove of trees. He crept along the side of the road and up to the edge of the woods. Crouching there, Lee could hear leaves and sticks cracking as the girls tramped toward him. He held back until they neared the boundary of the trees.

Jessie and Vikki slowed their pace, allowing Vikki to call 911. She whispered the details and their location as calmly as she could. "We're okay right now, but we aren't sure he has left."

"All right, we are sending a unit. Stay on the line if you can."

Jessie halted. "We will be leaving this wooded area in a few feet, then what?"

"I guess we should walk along the road, so the police or Jeremy can... Oh, run! Jessie. Run!" Vikki screamed.

Lee lunged forward and grabbed Vikki by the arm, pulling her close to his face, "I've got you now, you nosey witch!" he yelled and yanked her arm until she yelped in pain.

"Let me go!" Vikki clawed at his hand, but he twisted her arm tighter and slapped her hard across her face causing her to stumble and fall.

"I told you to keep quiet," he snarled.

Hearing Vikki's screams, Jessie turned back, grabbed a thick, broken tree branch from the ground, and charged at Lee from behind. She swung it with all her might and aimed it at Lee's head. The limb grazed the side of his face and fell to his shoulder with a thud. A thin line of blood trickled from his cheek. He stumbled but regained his balance and kicked violently at Vikki, who had struggled up from the ground. His foot plowed into her stomach, and she bent to her knees in pain. Spinning around, Lee sprang at Jessie and shouted, "I told you I would be watching you!" He wrestled her to the ground then swung back to Vikki, who was clawing and striking him from behind with her uninjured arm. Jessie seized the opportunity, grabbed the branch again, and this time it landed with a thud on Lee's back. He stood and lunged for Jessie, but Vikki kicked the back of his knee, and he fell forward cursing. Twisting his body, he caught hold of Vikki's foot and took her down with him.

At that instant, Lee was struck with such force that it propelled him forward into the trunk of a large tree. Dazed, he turned and tried to move forward but was hammered in his gut and fell back. "Leave her alone, you bastard!" Jeremy shouted as his fist struck Lee's jaw. Lee slumped against the tree, regained his footing, then aimed a weak hit toward his assailant. Jeremy ducked the blow and delivered another punch to Lee's midsection driving him to the ground. Lee staggered to his feet, cursing as blood seeped from his lip, and walloped Jeremy across his chest, knocking him off balance and bringing him to his knees. He sprang up, landed another blow to Lee's jaw, and heard a cringe-worthy crack of bone. Lee crumpled to the ground. Fueled by adrenaline and rage, Jeremy dragged Lee to his feet and pummeled him in his stomach. Lee buckled over and fell backward into the tree. Jeremy yanked him to his feet again.

Jordan, approaching the grove of trees from the other direction, raced toward the sound of yelling and burst onto the scene. "Jeremy! Stop! He's down." Jordan grasped his friend's arm and held his eyes, willing him to heed his warning. "It's over, Jeremy."

Jeremy's livid eyes studied his partner for a long moment, letting Jordan's truth soak into his raging thoughts, then he grudgingly let Lee slump to the ground.

Jordan surveyed the girls' injuries, "Are you girls okay?" His eyes grazed Vikki's limp arm, which she held gingerly. "Vikki, your arm looks bad. It may be broken. He looked closely at her swollen right eye. "You may have a black eye coming on."

Vikki held her limp arm close to her body and muttered. "Well, I've never had either, so there's that."

"Here, we have some supplies with us to make a sling. It is going to hurt a little, but it will feel better when I get your arm stabilized." Vikki grimaced as Jordan crafted a sling and secured her arm.

Jeremy gathered his composure and began to examine Jessie, bandaging an abrasion on her hand. "You're lucky. It doesn't look too bad. This should fix you up. Does anything else hurt?"

Jessie looked at him with her dirt-smudged face, "I bruised my knee, but I don't think anything is broken." She twisted her lips as she rose to her feet.

Jordan came over and felt Jessie's knee, agreeing that it wasn't a severe wound though it was discolored. "You girls helped do some damage to your adversary it seems," Jordan quipped, turning awed eyes to Lee still flat on the ground.

Barely able to control his loathing, Jeremy stomped over and knelt by Lee to attend to his wounds. He turned the injured man over to dress the cut on his face and observe his wounded jaw, but Lee swore and swept Jeremy's hand away. "Fine, have it your way," Jeremy said with disgust and threw the gauze back in his bag.

"Vikki will need my help walking to the car, so you are going to have to assist Lee, Jeremy." Jordan stated flatly.

Jeremy shot him a withering look. Reluctantly, he tended Lee's wounds, even as Lee cursed and writhed in fury. Jeremy pulled the defiant man to his feet and said with daggers in his voice, "Unless you want me to leave you here to rot, you'd better cooperate and let me help you to the road." Lee complied out of necessity as Jeremy supported him, and the battered group traipsed to Jessie's car waiting in the ditch.

The police had arrived on the scene and were searching the area from where they had received the distress call. An officer was examining Jessie's car. Jeremy yelled and waved, "We're over here."

Two policemen heeded his gesture and jogged up the field to meet them. After a briefing from Jordan, they took a mangled Lee into custody and left Jordan and Jeremy to take care of the girls.

"Well, this has been exciting. Is everyone still breathing?" Jordan said dryly. Except for her bruised knee and a few scratches, Jessie was not harmed, but Vikki's arm needed medical attention. "Let's get you to the ER, Vikki," Jordan offered with sympathy. "Does it hurt badly?" He held her as she stumbled along.

"It hurts, but I'm okay. Jeremy saved me from further injuries, I'm sure."

"I'll help her," Jeremy said and wrapped his arm around Vikki.

"Sure thing, Preacher Boy," Jordan's grin was broad.

"I'll be okay," said Jessie. "But I don't think we could have fought Lee off much longer."

"Well, you certainly slowed him down," Jordan assented.

Vikki tilted her head and looked up at Jeremy, "Why are you so quiet? You're our hero."

"I just did what any guy would do," he said as he swept his unruly hair from his face.

"You did great, Jeremy," Jordan tapped his arm, "You had it all under control. Let's go, guys. We'll call a tow truck in the morning."

Dawn was breaking when Vikki, her arm in a sling and on pain medicine, was released from the ER. Luckily, it was severely strained but not broken. Jordan and Jeremy headed back to the fire station after dropping the exhausted girls off at Vikki's house.

"You two girls sure put up a big fight," Jordan said. "Go get some sleep."

Jeremy's eyes were full. "I was so terrified when you called. I'm just glad you're both safe."

"Me, too, Jeremy. You guys saved us." Vikki answered.

"Just doing our job, ladies," Jordan winked and blew them both a kiss. "You need to get some rest now." Turning to Jeremy, who stood in a daze staring at Vikki, he nudged him with his elbow, "Say goodnight, Jeremy."

Jeremy pushed Jordan aside, not sure if he was irritated or amused. "Goodnight, girls."

The weary girls laughed, said their goodbyes, and shuffled into the house.

* * *

After Jordan parked the ambulance, the worn-out men sat at the table in the station's lounge to unwind before getting a few hours of sleep. "Well, Jeremy, you have proved capable of handling all types of situations, and I hope you have gained more confidence in your skills and ability to act quickly," Jordan said.

"Maybe, but I nearly lost control of my anger. You had to call me on that."

"Yeah, but we've all been there, Jeremy. That's part of being a team. Partners have a responsibility to each other, to observe one another's emotional state and keep each other grounded. You would have done the same for me." He rubbed his finger across the top of his lip, "Anyway, I think you would've stopped yourself. That's the kind of man you are."

"I know, I'm sure I would have, but I wanted to hit him one more time," Jeremy said.

Jordan gave a crooked smile, "Well, maybe I should have let you." His tone became serious, "Do you know why I had you tend to Lee's wounds and walk with him? I could've done it myself, you know."

Jeremy shrugged, "I assumed you were a bit angry with me."

Jordan shook his head, "No, Jeremy, I wasn't upset with you at all. You did what you had to do to stop Lee. I just wanted to humble you a little so that you'd remember why we do what we do. We assist people who are hurt. That's our calling. Someone else judges the actions and doles out the consequences. We can't be the ones to set things right."

Jeremy nodded, "I understand that, but I was so furious. And to be honest, for a moment I didn't care what happened to him."

"It's hard for me, too, especially in circumstances like we had today," Jordan replied. "Believe me, when I came on the scene I had a struggle with my emotions, too. Maybe I was protecting myself in some way by having you help Lee. I believe one of the most difficult directives of Jesus is to love our enemies, and sometimes we have the perfect opportunity to do that in our occupation."

Jeremy nodded, "I appreciate your openness and wisdom." His expression turned lighthearted. "You could be a minister, you know it?"

"Nah, Preacher Boy," Jordan chuckled, "That's your gig. I don't think the church could handle me."

* * *

Vikki slept until almost noon, waking to the aroma of bacon and eggs frying. Being careful of her arm, she pulled on jeans and a t-shirt and wandered into the kitchen, where Jessie was dishing up her food. "Hi," she said, "I hope you don't mind me making us a very late breakfast.

"Not at all. It smells delicious."

While eating, they rehashed the events from the evening before, then sat quietly, each absorbed in their thoughts.

After a while, Jessie clasped her hands together, "Oh, I have something to tell you," she said, her eyes glowing. "But I forgot in all the excitement. Jordan and I are engaged."

Vikki's mouth fell open in happy surprise, "That's wonderful! I am so happy for you. Jordan is a great guy."

"Yeah, I can't believe my luck," Jessie beamed. "But Jordan claims he's the lucky one. We looked at rings the other night. I gave him a couple of ideas, so I am really excited to see what he chooses."

"That is so fun, and I think you are both lucky; you're perfect for each other."

"So, what about you and Jeremy?" Jessie ventured.

"We're seeing each other."

"Is it serious?" Jessie asked, her smile hopeful.

"Yeah," Vikki answered, the color rising in her cheeks.

"That's great," Jessie remarked. "You are good for him, and I can tell he loves you by the way he gazes at you. I've felt that from the first time I met you when we played cards that night."

"Well, maybe, but he had some issues to deal with."

Jessie nodded her agreement and hugged Vikki warmly. "I could not have chosen a better girl for my brother."

CHAPTER TWENTY-SEVEN

Jeremy took a sip of his soda and reached for a brownie. "Thanks for letting us come over for a little while."

"We're always glad when you and Heather come to visit," said Beth looking across the table at her husband.

Richard nodded. "We love to see our granddaughter, and you, too, of course," he snickered, tapping Jeremy's shoulder.

Jeremy laughed. "Not too sure about that."

Heather reached for another brownie casting a sideways look at her father. "One more," said Jeremy, "Then you can get down and play."

Heather took a bite, "Mmm, Nana makes good brownies."

"Yes, she sure does," agreed her grandfather.

Heather finished her brownie and hopped down from her chair. "Come play with me, Nana." She tugged on her grandmother's arm.

Beth hugged her and said, "You go set up the doll house and I'll be there in a little bit, ok? I want to talk to your daddy for a few minutes." She looked at Jeremy, who gave a slight nod.

Heather scampered off to the playroom, and the three adults engaged in friendly conversation for a few minutes. Then Jeremy guided the conversation to the purpose of his visit to Shannon's parents.

"I wanted to talk to you about something," he said, clasping his hands on the table.

His expression caught their attention. "Of course," Richard said, "What is it, Jeremy?"

Jeremy inhaled, unsure how to begin. "I, uh," he avoided their eyes and squeezed his fingers together. "I've met someone." He looked up, not knowing what reaction his words would bring. "Her name is Vikki and she lives in the house where I rent my apartment. I wanted you to know."

Beth and Richard exchanged looks of surprise. Beth found her voice first. "Oh, Jeremy, that's wonderful. We've prayed you'd find someone to love again."

"We have, Jeremy, that's true," Richard added. "You're a young man. You need someone in your life." He wiped under his eye, "We know the pain you have felt because we've dealt with it, too."

Jeremy breathed a sigh of relief. "I wasn't sure how you would react." He paused while he gathered his emotions. "I truly loved Shannon, and I will never forget her. It's been a long road for me and I know it has been rough for both of you, too. I never thought I would be able to find love again, but God had different plans."

Beth stood up and walked over to Jeremy. "We have never doubted your love for Shannon. Here, give me a hug."

Jeremy stood and hugged Beth, whose eyes glistened with tears, "We love you, Jeremy."

They all sat down again, and Richard cleared his throat. "We know you loved Shannon, and we appreciate how you have kept us in Heather's life. You have done a great job with her."

"Thank you. That means a lot to me. And I will continue to make you a part of Heather's life. You are a blessing to both of us."

They talked for a few minutes more, and then Beth excused herself to find Heather while Richard and Jeremy went to the workshop to see Richard's latest projects. When it was time to leave, Heather hugged her grandparents, and Beth hugged Jeremy again. "You are like a son to us. We are so happy for you."

"And when you're ready, we would love to meet your lady friend." Richard said.

Jeremy was overwhelmed by their total acceptance of his announcement. He hadn't realized how much their approval meant to him. "I would love for you to meet her. She is a wonderful woman, and she already loves Heather."

* * *

The late December night was cold and starry, the type of night where your breath condenses into a cloud as it meets the chilled air. It was still and quiet; the air was crisp but not uncomfortable. Heather was sleeping, and Jeremy had persuaded Vikki to come out to the balcony, the place he had first kissed her, the night he had fallen in love. He marveled at how God did have plans for him after all and somehow brought him through suffering into something beautiful. Though Jeremy would never understand why Shannon died as she did, he could now accept it and rejoice that she now lived in heaven. Shannon and their innocent love would always be a treasured memory in his heart. Now, though, he stood beside the woman with whom he wanted to spend his life. She was beautiful inside and out. He shifted his feet and attempted small talk as he gathered his courage.

"How's Lisa handling all the things going on with Lee?" Jeremy questioned.

"Remarkably well, I'd say," Vikki replied. "Lisa is a strong woman. She filed for divorce, and Lee agreed to plead guilty to a battery charge against Jessie and me to avoid a harsh sentence. The court split their assets, and of course, Lee lost his partnership in the law firm. Lisa said he will spend some time in jail for attacking us." She looked out over the balcony. "Oh, and Lisa resigned her position to accept one in Terre Haute, where her sister and brother-in-law live. She is staying with them while looking for another place."

"And thanks to you, Lisa is a safe woman," Jeremy took her hand. "You saved her from years of abuse, maybe even saved her life."

"Oh, not really," Vikki said, her eyes glowing, "I was just her friend."

"You're wonderful, and I adore you." Jeremy said, "You are my best friend in the world and so much more. I can't believe you put up with all my doubts. I love you," he whispered.

"I love you too, Jeremy." Vikki's eyes shone.

Jeremy dug in his pocket and produced a small white box. "Here, this is for you. It reminds me of your beautiful green eyes."

Vikki took the offered box with shaky hands and fumbled, trying to open it. Jeremy steadied her hand and lifted the lid. An elegant oval cut emerald with a tiny diamond on each side set in a silver band met her eyes.

"Oh, Jeremy. It's beautiful." She pulled him close and kissed his lips. "I don't know what to say."

"Say, you love me." He lost himself in her eyes, "Say you will marry me and be a mother to Heather."

She gazed at the man she now loved. With his tousled dark blond hair and blue eyes, he looked nothing like her first husband. Jeremy was Tom's polar opposite in personality, too. Jeremy was kind, sensitive, and a man of integrity. Vikki smiled up at him.

"Yes, I will marry you. I love you, Jeremy Marcus, and I love Heather as my own daughter."

Jeremy drew her close and gently touched her lips with a slow, feather-like kiss. He needed her, wanted to be with her, and promised himself he would never hurt her, "I will never be unfaithful to you, Vikki. You will never know that kind of hurt again. Please believe that. God brought us together in a way I could never have imagined, but I am forever grateful He did."

Vikki wrapped her arms around his neck. "I trust you more than I have ever trusted anyone. I will always love you. You are my destiny."

Embracing her now, Jeremy's soul was free, released forever from its chains. God did have plans for him, and they were good.

* * *

Jeremy parked his car and walked with Heather to Shannon's gravesite. He smiled at the sight of the fresh flowers that adorned her headstone. They must be from Shannon's parents. He knew they frequently came, though he hadn't been here since Heather was an infant. Now that he had begun to deal with all his anger and guilt, it was time to come again.

"Look at the pretty flowers, Heather. You know how we talk about your mommy living in heaven with Jesus."

"Yes, we pray about her. She died, but now she is happy in heaven, right?"

Her look of innocent trust melted Jeremy's heart. "Yes, Angel, she's happy. See this stone? It has her name, Shannon, written on it. It marks her grave and helps us remember her."

"And we have pictures to help us remember Mommy, too." She pointed to the headstone. "I like the flowers."

Jeremy pulled his daughter close. "Heather, let's sit here and talk to Mommy for a minute."

"Can she hear us, Daddy?"

"I'm not sure, but I want to believe she can."

Heather was quiet for a second, then looked up at her father. "God hears us. So He can tell her what we said if she doesn't hear us."

Jeremy shook his head in wonder and kissed the top of her head. "Yes, Heather, I'm sure that's true. Anyway, I have something to tell her, ok?

"Ok, Daddy,"

Jeremy walked Heather closer and sat in front of the grave with her on his lap. He touched the letters on the stone and bit his lower lip. "Hey, Shannon," his voice was soft. "Look at our little girl. She is beautiful, like you, and she has your golden hair."

Heather sat quietly and snuggled against Jeremy's chest. "Do you want to say anything to Mommy?" Jeremy asked, but she lowered her eyes and shook her head. Jeremy held her tight. "It's ok, you can just listen."

Jeremy continued, "Anyway, I want you to know that I'll always love you, and," he hesitated choosing his words with care. "With God's help I've learned to accept what happened, and I've found someone to love again." A tear leaked over the lower rim of his eye. "I think you would like her. Her name is Vikki, and she loves Heather and me."

Heather raised her head at the mention of Vikki's name. "I love Vikki. Is that good?"

"Yes, Heather. I love Vikki, too. Come with me. I need to get something from the car." They rose and walked to the car. Jeremy gathered two red roses and a small vase from his front seat. "Your mommy loved red roses, so I bought two of them to put on her gravestone. One for me, and one for you."

"Can we put them with the other flowers?"

"Sure, let's do it. Do you want to set them on the top?"

Heather reached for the vase and set the flowers on the stone. "Our flowers are pretty, aren't they, Daddy?"

Jeremy knelt by his daughter and wrapped his arm around her shoulders. He gazed at the flowers and remembered his last visit to this place. "Yes, Angel, they are beautiful." He pulled her closer. "And best of all, they're not broken."

ABOUT THE AUTHOR

Broken Chains is Cynthia Terrell's debut novel. She taught elementary students for many years and continues to work with children at an after-school club. She and her husband Dave have two grown children and one granddaughter. *Broken Chains* is a story she has had in her heart for several years. Her new goal is a career in writing.

CPSIA information can be obtained
at www.ICGtesting.com
Printed in the USA
BVHW081529281221
625047BV00004B/196